Portrait of Deborah

Portrait of
Deborah

BY

FLORENCE CHANOCK COHEN

Julian Messner,   New York

Published simultaneously in the United States and Canada
by Julian Messner, a division of Simon & Schuster, Inc.,
1 West 39 Street, New York, N.Y. 10018.

Fifth Printing, 1967

Printed in the United States of America
Library of Congress Catalog Card No. 61-6368

Portrait of Deborah

One

"Deborah!"

Mother's voice echoed down the long hall to her room, where she stood in front of the oak-framed mirror viewing herself scrupulously.

"It's five minutes to eight, dear."

Don't I know it, she thought, remembering how she had opened her eyes and stared into the round face of the clock on her nightstand at six o'clock, then again at a quarter to seven, and finally at seven-fifteen she had crawled out of bed.

She tucked the cotton blouse into her skirt and squinted into the mirror. The snowy whiteness of the blouse blurred against the deep tan of her skin, and she told herself there is absolutely nothing like living in Chicago six blocks from Lake Michigan.

With long vigorous strokes she brushed the auburn pony tail, bringing it forward to catch the end that hung halfway to her waist. Then, locking the barrette securely, she swung the pony tail back, and after a last oblique glance, stood away. There—all ready now. She felt her finger tips cold and tingly with excitement. But how do you slow yourself down, persuade yourself that this morning is only the beginning of the senior year and not the night of scholarship awards?

She made a quick reeling turn, trying to catch the reflection of the wide green skirt in the mirror, but instead she landed against the footboard of her bed. Graceful as a dinosaur, she groaned, and nursed the stubbed toe against the other leg.

In the kitchen Mother had hot cocoa waiting, and Grandpa, at one end of the table, was bending over a tall glass of tea, blowing at the steam with concentration. He studied everything like that, being a scholar of detail and a master of precious observations. Grandpa even looked at his pocket watch with a kind of ritual, pulling it from his vest pocket and slowly raising it to his eyes while he opened the case with a deft snap of his finger. Deborah suspected that Grandpa enjoyed the cool feel of the gold watch, and that, while he held it, he had memories of all his past in Poland, where the watch was handed from father to son and was like a history of his people.

She plunked down opposite him. "Honestly I will never understand why this family needs hot brew by the first week of September. It's *warm* outside."

Grandpa's moist blue eyes brightened over the filmy glass, and he fingered his wisp of gray beard the way he always did before making a choice remark; but she anticipated him and, not caring to get involved with

8

epigrams this morning, promptly added, "Never mind. Enjoy yourself."

But Grandpa was not one to neglect opportunity. He bandied back in an English slurred with Polish and Yiddish accents. "Deborah, a warm stomach is the first step to contentment, thus to wisdom."

"Oh, Grandpa. That's awful."

She sipped the cocoa, made a face, and looked at her watch. "Gosh, it's eight-fifteen!" she said, making her voice sound deliberately harried as Mother put half a piece of French toast on her plate.

Thank heavens they're playing along this morning, she thought, letting me pretend it's not a full forty-five minutes before school starts. And Mother wasn't heaping her plate, which was a habit she had tried to endure quietly since her little brother, Danny, died of polio only a year before the vaccine was discovered. Then Mark went off to college, leaving Mother with only her to focus on.

But this was not the morning to analyze Mother. She could even finish the cocoa without feeling martyred, because today she would know. Today was like the overture to the scholarship and the Academy of Music. Oh, mind, mind, she protested to herself, don't dwell on it, pull the reins back, don't count your chickens. Now she sounded like Grandpa and, blowing a kiss in the direction of the kitchen, she was out of the house with Mother's words half-registering.

"Deborah! Come home on time, dear. There's something we have to tell you."

Outside, the street had a feel of excitation about it; even the elevated train, two blocks away, swished by more purposefully this morning as though it were accommodating a new pace. The school children had not yet come out, and the street was still quiet; but you would have to be made of granite not to sense the preparation and bustle behind the windows of the tall apartment houses. Autumn in the city was beginning its quicksilver vitality and soon the sprawling arteries of Chicago would refresh its flow; the pulse of the city would beat with music at Orchestra Hall, new exhibits at the Art Institute, and the streets of the Loop jammed with shoppers who had been waiting for cooler weather. Debby savored the thought of it. She had been born in Chicago, right here on the South Side, with the El train drowning out her first squeal, as Dad put it.

She walked briskly to the end of the block where her father's business, the Rose Pharmacy, had its awning out, and she went up close to the window. Dad was sitting at an ice-cream table engrossed in conversation with a rotund man who overflowed the chair and took up the small table with his briefcase and hat. Dad held a sheaf of papers in his hand, and the man, neatly dressed in a tan cord suit, kept nodding his head as though questions were tumbling at him with rapid fire. Mr. Rose looked up and noticed her; she didn't want to interrupt, but he was motioning her in.

He introduced Mr. Jackson, who was younger than he appeared from outside and who smiled good-naturedly when Dad said he was the City Planning Commission's early-rising star.

She thought he looked more like a whole constellation. "Dad," she managed to say without betraying her impression of Mr. Jackson, "I just wanted to ask—"

Before she could finish, Mr. Rose answered abruptly. "Not now Deb. We'll talk it all out tonight."

Talk what all out? What was the matter with everyone? First Mother so quiet; and now Dad, edgy. Usually it was the other way around.

"I only wanted some pencils. Nice soft ones—number two, I think."

Dad seemed relieved, and as he walked around the back of the counter she saw him shake his head at Mr. Jackson. The gesture was almost imperceptible but there was no mistaking it; Dad wanted Mr. Jackson to keep quiet about something. Well, whatever it was, it would have to wait. She planted a quick kiss on her father's temple and said good-by to Mr. Jackson, apologizing for her haste as she made for the door.

After three long blocks the flagpole at the entrance to Purcell High was at last visible. Such a weather-beaten old building, she thought. But it was part of the neighborhood's history; it had stood here for over fifty years. She was eager to get inside, to sense the musty-smelling halls that were washed down every Friday with strong soap and pine oil which lingered fresh and fragrant on Monday mornings. She remembered that this was Monday, and sniffed; then, catching herself, she laughed aloud.

11

Now the span of summer had been bridged and the beginning of school was a reality.

A tall boy planted himself in front of her, looking down with a dark, smiling handsomeness.

"What's so funny, little one?"

"Tony! You're back."

"In the flesh, little one. But weak, very weak, after counseling all those kids. Now what and who were you laughing about?"

She giggled softly. "Pine oil. It took us a whole half-semester to track down the smell."

"My, my," Tony clucked, shaking his head at her with mock concern. "The summer's gone hard with you, but fear not. Uncle Tony won't tell."

"Nitwit." She poked his arm gently. "I was remembering the smell of school on Monday mornings. Never mind, though. How was camp?"

Tony's face grew serious. "For me, it was terrific," he said. "Good experience, a chance for some exercise and pin money; but for the kids . . . well, you see, for them it's like a sliver of meat between two thick crusts of bread. They came from slums; they go back to slums, with a tiny whiff of fresh air in between."

"I know, Tony. But it's better than nothing, isn't it? And someday things might change. Don't get so grim about the world."

"Yeah, things will change." His voice was tinged with bitterness.

He's still hotheaded, she thought. Tony, the unbridled

colt with no stomach for being harnessed; but not without reason. It wasn't easy for Tony to see his parents work fifteen hours a day in their grocery store so their six children could eat and have clothes. Perhaps that was why Tony was so impatient with the world.

As they entered the school building, the animated din of the halls was too distracting for conversation and he turned in the direction of the stairway.

"I'm in peanut heaven this year," he called back. "See you at lunch."

Debby hurried to the bulletin board. There were still a few minutes before the bell to take a quick look at the announcements. Biting the inside of her cheek, she scanned the postings inside the glass-enclosed case; then she saw it:

THE W. H. TAYLOR ENDOWMENT FUND
FOR PURCELL HIGH SCHOOL GRADUATES
ANNOUNCES ITS 25TH ANNUAL SCHOLARSHIP
COMPETITION
FOR
STUDY AT THE NEW YORK ACADEMY OF MUSIC

She felt a chill go over her. New York Academy of Music, and for a thrilling moment she was already there, in a practice room alone, then with a distinguished teacher who was listening to her play; she could read his thoughts . . . promising pupil, promising artist.

The image jumped away at the shrill sound of the bell

and she turned dreamlike into the stream of students who were disappearing into rooms along the corridor. A voice behind slowed her down, and she turned to see Midge puffing and trying to catch up. Midge was plump and the boys teased her about not losing her baby fat; but she was known and widely admired for her brains, and for what she herself described as "my frankness and candor."

"Deborah Rose!" She pronounced the name as though issuing a decree. "I stopped at your apartment this morning. You didn't wait."

"Oh, Midge, I'm sorry. I guess I wasn't thinking about anything this morning."

"Nothing but that scholarship, you mean. I saw you at the bulletin board. Relax, Deb. Who would get the scholarship if not you? By the way, I heard the flagpolers talking about class officers. I heard your name in the air and it was bouncing high."

"Really, Midge? That never even occurred to me, not seriously anyway."

They found seats next to each other in Miss Thurston's old-fashioned room with the wide oak floor boards and the high ceilings, and after that it seemed as though each class session flowed into the other. By lunch time everyone around her in the cafeteria was groaning about schedules.

With a glistening eye, Midge unloaded peach pie à la mode from her tray. "Brain food," she said. "I'll need it for Chemistry IV."

Andrea Mescuto, Tony's twin sister, squeezed in beside

14

Midge at the already crowded table. "You know what I'd do for Chemistry IV if I were you, Midge?" she murmured. "I'd reduce. That Mr. Stone is Hollywood, absolutely Hollywood. I'll never understand why he stays a chemist."

Debby smiled to Jessie Perkins. She and Jessie could almost read each other's minds. They were old friends from Roosevelt Elementary and their common interest in music had strengthened the bond of friendship each year. Jessie's contralto was as powerful as all the other voices in the church choir put together. At least, that was her feeling when she visited the Negro Baptist Church to hear Jessie sing spirituals. Jessie had stood out from the others as a carillon from a dinner bell, and the vibrations of her voice when she sang "Swing Low, Sweet Chariot," rang in the church like the high chords of an organ. But Jessie could sing more than spirituals. She could sing Lieder in German and folk songs in Hebrew, and her ear for languages was as true as her pitch. She sat quietly at the table now, taller than most of the girls, her smooth, cocoa-colored face serene yet eloquently expressive. Watching her sit passively at the lunch table, who would suspect her of having such a gift?

Midge called, "Can you come into town after school? We need to bone up on fall fashion."

For all her plumpness Midge was more interested in fashions than anyone else in their group. Andrea, who was delicate, wanted more than anything to excel in a strenuous kind of modern dance rather than ballet, for which she seemed exquisitely proportioned, and Jessie spent more time working at the Settlement House after school than she did on practicing voice, which one only needed to hear to be convinced of its great promise. It made Debby wonder about herself too. She had felt a flush of pride and pleasure at Midge's telling her that she was being considered as a class officer. Of course it would be out of the question with the amount of preparation required for the Purcell competition; but it had a lure, a dimension of satisfaction even beyond that of her music—no, not beyond, but completely different, important in its own right. Curious.

"Well . . ." Midge repeated. "Fall fashion or no?"

"Sorry, Midge," Debby answered. "There's a great mystery at our house. Mum wants me home."

"Maybe you won the sweepstakes."

Tony sauntered up to catch Midge's last words. He opened his eyes wide and pretended surprise. "*Who* won the sweepstakes?"

Midge kept a straight face. "Debby," she answered. "The Roses are enormously wealthy."

"I don't believe it," said Tony. "Debby is a beautiful genius; and beautiful geniuses waste with consumption, or expire from love—they are never prosperous."

Debby laughed, waved them all away, and, balancing her tray, made for the exit. Despite her pretense at light-heartedness, pinches of worry had been coming and going inside her all morning. *Something* was troubling Dad. Why did he motion to Mr. Jackson to be quiet? And

16

what did Mother have to tell her? Could it concern Mark? What could the City Planning Commission have to do with Mark? It was something else. Yet, if Mark were safe at the University of Wisconsin, what was there to worry about? After all, they were all hale at home. And that was the most important thing—to their family anyway. For an instant she had a painful image of little Danny, just four years old, lying still and helpless, and, afterward, Mother's long road back to laughter, her tall figure stretched to its full height once more after it had seemed that she would shrivel in the chair by the bedroom window. What had it required of Mother to get up from that chair, remove the crib from the little room and replace it with a chintz-covered day bed? But she had had Dad, and Grandpa, her father, to help her.

Even so, she was too nervous about everyone's health, especially Mark's. Mark was robust as a race horse but, according to Mother, the University of Wisconsin was deliberately inducing malnutrition. When they went to visit him there, taking a meal in the cafeteria, Mother had passed through the food line scrutinizing it and eying the woman behind the counter with an I'm-an-agent-from-the-Pure-Food-and-Drug-Commission look. She finally chose for herself a small dish of cottage cheese mottled pink from a lonely-looking maraschino cherry, and when they were seated she sighed deeply at the sight of Mark guzzling a brown, cornstarchy concoction with apparent zest. When they arrived home again, Mother had hardly removed her hat when she started packing a carton: dried

17

fruits, nuts, Boston brown bread, and a hard salami—just for taste, she said. A large box of multiple one-a-day vitamins was thrown in and the package was shipped off the same day. Within a week Mark wrote to say that the salami was out of this world.

During her music hour with Mr. Mason, Debby managed to forget everything but the piano keys in front of her and Mr. Mason, a gaunt, youngish, and somewhat rumpled-looking man with long legs that he crossed and stretched out in front of him while he tipped his chair back precariously. Once, when his feet were stretched out like that, she noticed the sole of his shoe, badly in need of repair, and remembered Tony telling her that teachers starved. Starvation seemed to go with Mr. Mason and, whereas the actual thought of him starving was unthinkable, the idea of it enhanced his charm no end. He was a true inhabitant of the South Side's Hyde Park district: cosmopolitan, intense, slightly Bohemian and undeniably capable, even in the face of famine. Where Tony was incensed by the injustice of it, she was magnetized by its ascetic romanticism. To her, Mr. Mason, torn shoes and all, was the embodiment of devotion to art.

He wanted to see how she had kept up through the summer and she chose a Chopin ballade to play for him. It was one of her favorites, beginning with slow, lyric measures like the curtain going up on a green field at twilight. The theme was repeated with variations of minor chords building steadily, then shifting to a major

18

key and, with crescendo, returning to the opening theme for a thundering climax. At the end she had to snap herself back to the bright classroom, but Mr. Mason's voice, ringing with frank enthusiasm, was quick refreshment.

"Beautiful, Debby. Beautiful. You've hit those keys over the summer. I can see that, all right."

"Thank you, Mr. Mason." She hesitated. Should she ask him about the scholarship application? She did not want him to think she was pushing, but she had to know; she had waited so long. "Mr. Mason . . ." she began again, but as though he were clairvoyant he walked briskly to his desk and withdrew a manila envelope from under a pile of papers.

"Better take a look at this," he said, smiling. "We've got eight months yet, but I think you'll have to learn a concerto." His thick eyebrows went up as though it would help him to study her. "Hard work ahead, Debby. Are you up to it?"

She felt submerged in warmth and heard her voice sound almost shrill. "Am I up to it? I've been waiting all summer for today!"

Mr. Mason smiled again, and his sensitive eyes regarded her fondly. He murmured, "The Academy will be glad to get you," and then, with a teasing sternness, he added, "And keep those jazz sessions to a minimum, understand?"

She held up her hand. "My solemn promise."

She took the envelope and started toward the door, but

19

Mr. Mason called her back. He said, using her full name playfully, "Deborah. We won't get too solemn, will we?"

They both laughed.

All the way home the smooth manila envelope pressed against her fingers as though it were alive, and the sound of Mr. Mason's voice reverberated. She had avoided walking home with anyone so she could be alone, run his words over and over in her mind: "The Academy will be glad to get you" . . . glad to get you . . . glad to get you. Oh, but it was a gorgeous world and Mr. Mason was part of what made it so, and she would never forget him as long as she lived. If someday she should become a great pianist and reporters should ask her to whom she owed her distinguished career, without a moment's hesitation she would say, To a teacher on the South Side of Chicago, a fellow with holes in his shoes, a great soul who faced starvation so he might encourage young artists—Donald Mason of Purcell High School.

The wind was in her eyes and it felt as though the lake, about seven blocks away, was working itself into a storm. But who cared? Autumn was the time for storms, wasn't it? Each thing in its time, and soon it would be hers. She had to stop off at the drugstore and tell Dad.

The awning had been pulled back, and as she approached she could see that the lights inside were off. On the frame of the door a neat sign was thumbtacked: CLOSED.

$\mathcal{T}wo$

Debby burst into the apartment feeling as though someone had pushed her from behind. The sign CLOSED was the final stroke to a morning that had percolated with cues. And now Mother, Dad, and Grandpa sat huddled around the kitchen table. The same paper Dad had been holding at the store was spread out in front of them.

She tried to keep her voice casual, almost flippant. "Say, what's the idea of closing up at this hour, Dad?"

They had not even heard her in the hall, for they looked up now in complete off-guard surprise.

"Deborah!" Mother gasped. "You should call when you come in."

"For heaven's sake! I practically tore the door from its hinges. What *is* going on?"

Dad's eyes looked tired and bluish around the lids as though it were nights since he had slept well. He sat with his legs crossed, bent over, holding a pencil between his fingers like a cigarette. "Deb," he said, "come sit down with us. Mum will make you a sandwich."

21

She felt like a wind-up toy as she moved to the table, answering mechanically, "Just milk, please."

Dad leaned over and picked up a folded paper from the floor at his feet and spread it out in front of her. It was a map of Chicago's South Side. She could sense him studying her face while she looked at it. Then he began talking rapidly.

"Our drugstore is located right here." He drew a heavy X at the spot on the map while Mother planted the milk in front of her and pressed her shoulder gently as she stood listening to Dad. Grandpa puffed at a cigarette from his tiny ivory holder. "You can see, Deb," Dad continued, "the new highway designed to intersect with the toll road will directly cross our corner. The businesses and apartments on this whole block will have to be razed."

Her long groan of relief brought a smile to Grandpa's face. "Is that all! Goodness, I was conjuring all sorts of stuff." She stopped short then, and whistled softly through her teeth. The realization struck her like the jolt at reaching the bottom of a slide. "That . . . that means this apartment too, doesn't it?"

"Debby"—Dad's voice was very gentle—"you should know right away, before I lead you on. We'll have to leave the neighborhood. Nothing was definite until this morning, and even then there was a chance we could resettle in this area."

She felt the color drain from her face although she could not fully grasp Dad's meaning. He was trying to say something important—something that would change her life completely, something all settled now and irrevocable. Her fingers tingled from clutching the manila envelope Mr. Mason had given her, and she heard Dad's voice like an echo, hollow and distant, as he repeated, "It's a terrible shame you started at Purcell this morning. I'm so sorry we let you—"

"What do you mean you're sorry I started at Purcell? What does it have to do with Purcell?"

"Sweetheart, we're moving to North Haven in about four weeks. You must have heard of it. It's that pretty place up the lake, forty miles from here. I had a drugstore lined up—"

The words caught then, cold in the pit of her stomach, and she heard herself breathe, "North Haven?"

"Debby, dear, if the decision of the Planning Commission had been different you would never have known a ripple of disturbance. If we're guilty of anything, it's trying to protect you too much. We looked everywhere for another business and apartment in this neighborhood. You know how overcrowded it is. It's just not suitable any longer."

His words would not seem to settle down in her mind. North Haven . . . North Haven. That pretty place up the lake. Something about the City Planning Commission. Then she heard her own voice, almost a shriek, "Suitable! For whom? Did you ask me about that?"

She flashed the manila envelope in front of them. "Do you know what's in here? My scholarship application to the Academy in New York. Mr. Mason said they'd be glad to get me."

The three of them seemed to be dancing before her eyes. She spurted from the chair, almost knocking it over, then stopped to straighten it. It couldn't be irrevocable. They wouldn't do such a thing without consulting her first. She wasn't a child, after all, and they had always asked her opinion on family matters. They wanted to discuss it with her. That was all.

"I don't think we should do it," she said. "I'm in my senior year, and all. And the scholarship . . . it's my big chance." She emitted a rasping little laugh. "You don't get chances like that every day."

Dad's eyes were lowered and he kept retracing the X he had marked out on the map. She saw the lines grow heavy and thick while his voice slowed and its tone softened.

"Darling," he whispered, "it's done. I wish . . . I . . ."

Mother's arm was around her shoulder; but she yanked away and, as she turned, into her glance the three of them shot swiftly, Dad's eyebrows knit; Mother's face pale; Grandpa sitting quietly, leaning on his elbow with his hand spread over his cheek.

She closed the door of her room and leaned back against it; she saw the oak-framed mirror, the hairbrush resting quietly on the bureau, and remembered that she had not cleaned the hair out of it this morning. It was such an excited, absent-minded morning. She went to get the hairbrush and realized then that the manila envelope was still in her hand. She dropped it to the floor and picked up the hairbrush, rubbing her palm into the bristles. She wanted it to hurt so she could feel something.

On the edge of her bed she sat staring at the braided rug, tracing it around and around to the red center where it reached its starting loop. Her eyes were beginning to sting from staring at the rug; and the palm of her hand was hot, as though it had been burned. She heard the hairbrush drop to the floor; her face was in her pillow and she was hardly breathing.

The scholarship was gone. Only Purcell graduates were entitled to compete for it, and now she could not have it. After five years of hard work and hope, she would not be eligible. They were moving within a month —moving away from the city; away from Midge and Jessie, Tony and Mr. Mason, everyone she loved. The scholarship was gone, gone, gone. She would never forgive them for taking her chance away. As long as she lived she would never forgive them.

Mother's voice directly above her called softly, "Deborah"; but she would not look up.

"Debby? Please, dear. It's only fair to hear us out. If there were the least chance of settling in this neighborhood again, you don't think we would have uprooted you, do you, dear? But it turned out that you'd have to leave Purcell anyway, and its about half the risk for Dad to locate where neighborhoods don't change so rapidly. You've always been so sensible."

25

It was at Mother's last word, "sensible," that she felt she would explode. "Good old Debby, the brick," she garbled back. "You pull every prop from under me and you expect me to be a brick. I've lost my scholarship. It was everything I wanted, and I lost it because you and Dad didn't care."

Mother's hand was stroking her hair, and she wished suddenly she could bury her head in Mother's shoulder the way she did when she was small; but she couldn't do it. She could only lie there listening to Mother's urging voice, as though it were a wall between them.

"Baby," Mother went on, "you know in your heart that isn't true. I know how much it must hurt to lose the scholarship. But no one can take away your music, darling." Her voice lowered to almost a whisper. "I lost something too, once," she said. "It takes time and it isn't easy."

She lay very still. It was one thing, she thought, to be helpless against circumstances like Danny's death; but it was another thing to cause them, to destroy something in cold blood. No, there was nothing she could answer that she wouldn't be sorry for. It was better not to talk at all. Only one thing was certain. Mother and Dad had done this to her. No matter how they might rationalize, the real truth would stand and no one could change it.

There was a cool place now on her arm where Mother's hand had been. She heard the bedroom door click shut and she was glad to be left alone in the fluid darkness of the pillow.

The following day, she waited until just before school let out to go back for her belongings and transfer. It was the thing she dreaded most, since last night's supper when they had all sat soberly at the table except for Grandpa's attempts to liven things up. Dad had tried to explain that they were losing something too, and that he and Mother had been in this neighborhood for over eighteen years and it would not be easy to start over, to build the same reputation in a new place. The venture could be disastrous for all of them, and more so if they didn't pull together. Yet she could not forgive them or squelch the hot feeling that came in waves with each thought of the lost scholarship.

But there was not much time for thoughts. The opening of school in North Haven was in three weeks and, although Dad had a drugstore already lined up out there and several good houses for consideration, there were endless decisions to be made. North Haven—it might as well be on the other side of the moon for all the reality it held. Mother had described it as "perfect," with the lake and beach stretching the length of the town and the tall elm trees forming graceful arches over the streets. She had looked almost young as she spoke of it.

"It has a lovely small-town atmosphere, Deborah," she said. "You'll come to like it, I know. And just think! The El won't wake us up at six in the morning. You will give it a chance, won't you, dear?"

She had not answered except for a nod of her head. Did they really think she could jump from one life into another, give up everything for trees and a strip of beach? Did they think she was that simple-minded?

She approached the entrance to Purcell with feet like lead. If only she did not have to face them; if it were possible to disappear without ever saying good-by! She would have to tell Mr. Mason. There was a quickening of hope at the thought of him. What if he said she could compete for the scholarship anyway? Even if she didn't graduate from Purcell? What if he said, Deborah, I know what it means to want music, to love art, and I won't let this happen to you. You don't think I'd see my prize student lose her big chance, do you? Never you mind, Deborah Rose, it will be all right. Perfectly all right.

By the time she reached the entrance to Purcell she could walk through the door without wincing. She was sure that Mr. Mason, the teacher who had holes in his shoes for art's sake, who had suffered for it, would not let a little technicality interfere with her career.

His room was very quiet when she went in, and for a moment she did not see him. Then his dark head appeared over the desk in the corner of the room, and he straightened up and smiled.

"I always put the important things in the bottom drawer, and then I can't find them," he laughed. "Well, Debby. I'll bet you have that application all filled out."

Her insides quivered while she scolded herself. Don't you cry. Don't you dare cry. "Mr. Mason . . ." Her voice behaved. "I didn't open it . . . not because I didn't want to, but there wasn't any purpose—you see, we're moving away. The highway is cutting through our neighborhood, and Dad couldn't find another suitable place; so we're going to North Haven and, you see, there wasn't any use . . ."

She couldn't go on watching the surprise on his face, his hands quickly slung into his pockets, and the sudden stoop of his shoulders. It would be, oh, so much easier if he said she wasn't likely to get the scholarship anyway, that it was better to scratch out now before the real disappointment.

Instead his voice sounded low and heavy with surprise. "What! When did this happen?"

That did it. She slumped to a desk chair and cried, feeling the long pony tail soft across her knees.

She was relieved when Mr. Mason finally spoke. "I'm not sure I understand all of it yet," he said. "Won't you tell me? You know I'll help if I can."

There. He had said it. He was going to help her. She swung the pony tail to her back and blotted her eyes with a tissue. "I'm terribly sorry, Mr. Mason. I promised myself I wouldn't do that." And then she told him everything.

When she finished he went slowly to the piano and turned away, lightly tapping the highest G on the keyboard while he stood thoughtfully. The air was filled with vibrations of the throbbing note and then she saw him shake his head.

"I wish there were something I could do," he said,

29

facing her now. "Do you know how the Purcell scholarship was established?"

"A man by the name of Taylor, wasn't it? He went to Purcell."

"Yes. He left the money in trust with a bank and I'm afraid he made a rigid stipulation that the award must go to a graduate of this school. The bank is in New York and I'm certain they wouldn't break such a rule, even if Mr. Treacher and myself tried to interfere."

Her heart was beginning a steady thump. The feel of it was absorbing. Funny, how it was the heart that reacted first and then the mind. Something about oxygen, or was it adrenalin? She hadn't listened well in biology class. No wonder she pulled a B in it, after all. This talk with Mr. Mason wasn't going right. Thump, thump, thump. She'd look it up someday.

Mr. Mason shook his head again. "A trust fund like the Taylor is pretty impersonal, Deborah. The machinery isn't set up for exceptions."

Machinery. He was on machinery, too. Impersonal machinery. She had to answer him. "Oh," she said, hearing it come out small and hoarse. She wanted to say good-by to him now, quickly, before he could sympathize with her, before she started crying again.

Her eyes met his hard stare. "Now listen here, young lady," he said. "You've lost your scholarship, but you haven't lost your talent. You don't think I've given you extra hours every week to see you throw it away."

She could find no answer. Any words now would be

trite and meaningless. She wanted to thank him for the extra hours, for all the love she had for him, for his caring now; but she couldn't. She couldn't trust herself to look at him again.

"Debby?" His voice sounded unfamiliar. "Do you think there's only one scholarship in the world? Only one way to become what you want to be?"

She felt suddenly tired. "That's what Grandpa said," she replied flatly. "He's wonderful at bolstering people."

"But it's true. We can still work together. It's only a short train ride from North Haven."

"That's nice of you, Mr. Mason. I do appreciate . . ." She had to get out of here while she could still find voice to remain civil. "I—I have to go now," she said. "My mother wants me to start packing dishes." She murmured a quick good-by and was out of the room before he could answer.

The halls were deserted when she left the office with her transfer, and she hurried to her locker.

She took out her gym shoes, the three books she had gotten from yesterday's classes, and the schedule card taped inside the door. Midge's voice at her shoulder made her jump.

"I zigzagged after you all the way from the office," she said.

Debby busied herself with brushing out the inside of the locker. She had not counted on seeing Midge yet. When Midge came by the apartment this morning she had waited in the bedroom while Mother explained.

Hearing Midge's unbelieving "Oh" had increased her own misery and now she dreaded seeing any of her friends.

Midge stood in back of her and she finally found courage to face her and say "Hi." It was odd seeing Midge looking this way, strained and fiddling with the strap of her purse. Midge was always buoyant about everything, as though she were riding the tail of a kite.

"You've heard about it, haven't you, Midge?"

"I stopped by your apartment this morning and you weren't even up yet. Your mother told me. Oh, Deb . . . I . . . ." Her voice trailed off.

"It won't have anything to do with our friendship, you'll see. North Haven is only up the lake. What's forty miles between us, Midge?"

"North Haven." Midge pronounced it like an oath. "Why didn't they tell you? They might at least have let you in on it."

"They were protecting me." She giggled. "Can you imagine that? It's actually funny when you think about it. I was being protected."

Midge looked at her curiously. "Well, I'd be furious if it were me. I'd raise the roof. Oh, Deb, I just can't stand it!"

For a moment they were quiet while Midge scrutinized the floor, her manner hesitant. "There's more you should know about North Haven," she began slowly. "I'm not sure if I should tell you; but you're the best friend I ever had, and I won't let you walk into that snake pit without warning you."

Taken off guard, Deborah felt as though someone had pulled a drawstring inside her.

Midge recaptured her old intensity. "My cousin Frances, the one at the University of Illinois now . . . well, she went to North Haven High. There's only one high school there—"

"It's only a small suburb."

"Narrow suburb, you mean."

"Oh, Midge, what is it?" As soon as she asked, she was sorry. What about North Haven could possibly make any difference? And if it were something devastating she didn't want to know about it; risk was deepening the cavity of hurt inside her. But it was too late. The words were pouring out of Midge like a ball of yarn unraveling downhill.

"When I say narrow, I mean *narrow*. Frances told me that the girls at North Haven High make a game of cutting people to size. They have clubs out there, exclusive clubs, and I'm scared to death they'll hurt you."

The drawstring pulled tighter. "They don't even know me."

"Don't they? Wait until they see your grandfather. They'll know all they want to. In North Haven the only experience with long beards and foreign accents they've had is in cartoons. I almost feel sorrier for your grandfather—"

"Sorrier for Grandpa! Since when is Grandpa a freak?"

Midge's face colored. "I didn't mean it that way, Deb. You know how much we all love Grandpa. But North Haven's different—they're narrow and prejudiced."

33

So that was it. North Haven did not like foreigners or Jews. Midge had taken the long way around to say it, but it couldn't matter less. And in a way it was a relief to know that she wouldn't have to force herself—make herself like them, or them like her.

Midge looked agonized. "I only wanted to warn you so you could go in armed," she said. "Frances told me how hard it was for her, how the girls were competitive and nasty, and how you couldn't really be yourself. Now I've upset you. Oh, why can't I keep my big mouth shut?"

Deborah's sense of hollowness was complete. None of it made sense. From yesterday till now was like a vague amorphous cloud. What was there to say?

"Debby?" Midge's voice was almost a whisper. "Are you angry with me?"

"No . . . of course not, Midge. You only wanted to help. But there's nothing to be helped, is there?"

"Don't say that." Midge said. "If I know Deborah Rose, she'll make a hit anywhere. Can I come home with you? Do you need help with the packing?"

"Not now, Midge. I have an appointment. Come by tomorrow, maybe?"

They walked outside together and then she said goodby and turned in the opposite direction. She could not pinpoint the exact moment when she had made the decision; the closest she could come was when Midge said North Haven wouldn't allow you to be yourself. She had answered silently then, like taking a vow, that

North Haven would never know what her true self was. She would never reveal it to them.

The events of the past two days were like a razor-edge cleaving of everything she had known and hoped for. The change was like turning over a record for a new tune and, although it was pressed to the same disk, it had no relationship to the other side. She had to make it complete.

In front of Lacy's Beauty Salon she hesitated, then stopped and just stood there. After a moment she was inside asking the receptionist if they had time for a short-bob haircut.

The chic young woman with black hair piled high in a chignon cocked her head to one side.

"I'll get fired for discouraging business," she said. "You don't really want to cut that gorgeous pony tail, do you?" She put her hand to her own thick bun at the top of her head. "It's not real, you know. It would take years to grow mine to your length." She sighed. "You really want to cut off that rust-colored hair?"

"Yes," Debby breathed. "I want to. Do you have time now?"

The receptionist studied the appointment book while biting the end of her pencil. "Yep. Molly's free." She was matter-of-fact now, as though she had exercised great integrity and, having been rejected, returned to routine duties.

She got up and motioned for Debby to follow. Almost at the end of the long line of booths, she called, "Molly, you have a customer for a three-inch cut."

Three

When Mother saw her that evening after the haircut, her lips quivered before she emitted the name "Debby?" and she blinked as though a gauzy apparition had appeared. Dad yanked off his glasses and scratched behind his ear with the stem. Then they both asked "Why?" at once, and when she answered simply "Time for changes, isn't it?" they exchanged glances, and Mother declared the style lovely on her. Dad nodded agreement and finally, on not so subtle cues from each other, they dropped the matter completely. Getting the china packed was the matter at hand.

But Grandpa had studied her, staring quietly for a long moment so that the cropped auburn ringlets tingled next to her scalp and their shortness beamed like radio waves, three inches, three inches, as though a tape measure were tacked inside her head.

"A marvelous act of anger," he had said, "If only . . ."

"If only what?" she had managed to mumble back, annoyed.

"If only you could keep it from growing," he had sighed, smiling.

A pox on logic, she thought. The haircut had served its purpose and down deep she did feel different, at least— miserable, with an image of herself from Molly's mirror too incomprehensible to digest at once: auburn ringlets close to her head; blue eyes looking lost in a smallish, pointed face; the straight nose more of an exclamation point. Altogether a new Debby, she thought, not bad, then terrible—which was, after all, the heart of the matter.

Mercifully, however, for the next week there was little time to dwell on either the haircut or her friends. It was the first time the family had moved, and Debby was immersed in odd china, bric-a-brac, outgrown clothing, picture albums, folders of odd shapes and sizes that Mother had accumulated over the years. She suggested and then she *pleaded* that Mother should take this opportunity to throw things away; but after looking each thing over with a ponderous air ending in a sigh, Mrs. Rose relegated everything she could not use to boxes marked "Miscellaneous."

The apartment assumed a naked look after the rugs were rolled up. When Midge came, the morning the floors were laid bare, she whistled softly through her teeth. "Is this the same place?" she asked.

"I don't think so," Debby answered, sprawling in a chair with her legs slung over the arm. "There's nothing left of it, is there? I can't imagine ever having lived here."

"I know," said Midge. "Remember the party you gave last summer? This old living room was sure lived in then—you had that piano going like a hot tap dance."

"Don't," Debby answered, swinging her legs over and getting up. "I don't want to think about it. What's gone is gone and I really don't care any more. As far as I'm concerned, I'm going along for the ride. Want a coke, Midge?"

In the kitchen Midge observed her with a squinty-eyed scrutiny.

"Not bad," she said.

"What?"

"The haircut. You look cute—tousled, sort of."

"I don't want to talk about that, either."

"Okay," Midge answered after a long pull on her coke. "Let's talk about the party we're giving you. Tomorrow night. My house."

Debby clicked the refrigerator shut and stood with her back to Midge for a moment. When she turned and saw Midge's sympathetic face and warm half-smile, she could not keep her feelings back any longer.

"Oh, Midge, that's wonderful of you," she said, and began sniffling back tears. "I don't know if I can stand it; I'll die."

"You won't die," Midge said. "Gosh, you're a heroine— I wish something like this would happen to me; the only attention I get is when I've got the virus."

"Sure," Debby answered, "I feel sorry for you. Hey!" She snapped her fingers, remembering that they were moving the morning after the party. "I'll bet they won't let me go," she said glumly.

"Why not?"

"Moving day the next morning."

"So? My goodness, Deb, your folks didn't turn into monsters overnight."

"Didn't they?" Debby asked fliply.

The party was not the same as when the gang got together other times; it had overtones of a wake at first, and even after it got going she had to force herself to keep up and make it worth their trouble.

Andrea, Tony's sister, had been intensely interested in North Haven High since she had heard about their having a modern dance group.

"Wish I were going," she said. "The only thing you get in the way of dance at Purcell is chin-ups in the gym."

"Who spoke those disloyal words?" Midge asked while passing cokes.

"Phooey," Andrea said. "Purcell ought to be more progressive. Why couldn't they sponsor a dance teacher?"

"Because," Tony answered, "they have no m-o-n-e-y. Ever heard of it?"

"That's all I ever do hear around here," Andrea answered soberly. "I wish I were going to North Haven, like Deborah, the lucky duck."

"I'll gladly change places," Debby said, "in a minute.

39

If what you want is at North Haven, what I want is at Purcell. Isn't it crazy how people can't ever get what they want?"

"Hey!" Binky Jones interrupted. "Cut the gloom. This is supposed to be a party. Where's the music, Midge?"

"Phonograph's busted," Midge called back from the kitchen. "Debby will have to play."

Debby winced when she heard Midge say it, as though an exposed nerve were touched. When she had the haircut she had decided not to play any more; that part of her life was over. She had worked hard and hoped hard, but all the pieces had blown away and she could not reconstruct them. The sound of music was enough to shrivel her insides and the memory of herself playing triggered a new, strange reaction—she wanted to escape from the imagined sounds of the piano; to hold her hands hard over her ears, and run.

"Come on, Debby, give us the cool heat," Andrea said, while everyone got up from sitting tailor-fashion on the floor, ready to dance. Only Jessie Perkins stayed put watching Debby with a pensive air that clearly said she understood.

Debby wiped her moist palms with her handkerchief while she glanced furtively from Jessie's sober dark face to the animated forms of her friends waiting to dance. She couldn't pull a temperament act here; these were her closest friends and to hold back on them now would only queer things for the evening and, furthermore, she couldn't stand them pitying her. She had to play; there was no getting out of it, but tonight would be the last time; this was her swan song and she might as well whoop it up.

She took off her wrist watch, flexed her fingers, and sat down on the bench. She started a slow bass with a steady rhythm, repeating it over and over and then quickened the tempo, combining it with the melody of the treble which was twice the speed of the bass. Andrea and Tony, who danced together like professionals, were in the middle of the floor; Tony twirled her, and Andrea twirled, shaking her shoulders, and together they kicked out an up-to-date version of the Charleston; then Debby abruptly changed the rhythm to that of a mamba and instantly Tony and Andrea picked it up, Tony hunching his tall slim frame like a flamenco dancer while Andrea, her head erect, her slender arms poised in the air, followed him to the long catlike rhythms of the dance. Debby changed again, this time to samba, and Tony and Andrea jutted forward and back as though they had anticipated the new beat. The others stood back, some snapping their fingers, the rest clapping in rhythm, and then suddenly Tony broke from Andrea, pulled Jessie into the middle of the floor, and with the command "Sing, Girl," gave her a gentle shove toward the piano. Jessie began to hum the last bars of the samba and Debby changed to a tune Ella Fitzgerald had made popular. Jessie's deep contralto voice was perfect for it, and as she stood there, tall and serene, singing blues, Debby wondered for a moment if Jessie would ever get her chance, if she too felt that the fates were against her for the senseless reason that she was a Negro.

Nothing makes sense, Debby thought while she played. When the song was over and everyone applauded, she thought she was done with it, finished; but Sophie, Marv, Tony, and Midge insisted she give them one last number, a classical one this time. She turned back to the piano and without thinking started the Chopin ballade; but as though the nerve were pressed once more, she changed quickly to the "Minute Waltz." Her fingers flew beneath her eyes and suddenly everything seemed misty, as though the barometer inside her had plunged to the lower limits of safety. When, oh, when, would she be here with them again, and when would she play again, and when would she ever be happy? The barometer needle jiggled and signaled the words NEVER, NEVER, NEVER.

Four

A week later, in the new drugstore, Debby ran a cloth over the glass top of the showcase, wiping away the powdery pinkish film of dried cleaning fluid. It was the last showcase, thank heavens. She had been working on them all evening; her arms were tired and her head ached from inhaling the malodorous ammoniated stuff that was supposed to make plate glass like crystal. Mother and Dad would be finished in the stockroom tonight, and tomorrow morning the Rose Pharmacy of North Haven would open. It was a tidy place, contrasting sharply to the South Side store. Funny, she thought, how she had taken the old place for granted, the dust, soot, assorted varieties of grime that you chalked up to industry and progress; then you saw something different, and the things you knew and loved before were painfully revealed. The North Haven Pharmacy showed up the South Side store and flaunted its prettiness like a young girl might to a disheveled old woman.

A marble-topped soda counter occupied one side of the store and on the other side were booths, a juke box, a cigarette and sundry counter, and magazines. The prescription department was off by itself in a back alcove, which probably pleased Dad and made him feel professional—or at least, she thought, it would if she were he. Darned if she would go to college for four years just so she could sell licorice. It wasn't as though you had to gather herbs. But Dad accepted routine in life, was content with dullness and, she even suspected, enjoyed it. The way he had arranged the patent-medicine bottles, dusting each one and placing it at an exact spot on the shelf, was as though he were adjusting a painting to catch the light properly. She did not remember him so fastidious in the old store; but then, this was North Haven, where everything was pat and prissy. What she had seen so far she had registered with no more emotion than a camera: the wide clean streets, the symmetrically trimmed privet hedges, the tastefully dressed shoppers in supermarkets—all were flat against the canvas.

But Mother seemed deliriously happy. "Can you imagine?" she exclaimed at least once a day. "A gourmet shelf at the supermarket?"

The change in her was astonishing. In less than a week she was transformed from a nervous, preoccupied person to a cheerful youngish woman who clicked ideas for the new house and store, one after another.

It appeared that Mother had really hated the South Side all these years and was glad to be out of it. She had referred to it as dirty several times now, and said she had not realized the full pleasure of sunshine in eighteen years. Her contempt for the beloved old neighborhood was sheer treason.

But it was Grandpa who stayed the same throughout the move. He was sitting back in the little alcove now, stamping gum labels with the pharmacy's new address. She watched the slow deliberate movements of his arm as he stamped the small white squares as though it were not a tedious job but a scientific problem to be worked out each time. In contrast, she had rubbed the glass cases with quick, short strokes until her muscles hurt, but Grandpa's movements were relaxed and rhythmic. He was probably thinking about something; you could tell by his face. He stopped a moment and rubbed his bearded cheek with his finger and she remembered how snow-white and full his beard once was, but each year it had thinned and turned more yellowish. She felt a sudden pang. Would Midge's predictions about North Haven and Grandpa come true? No one had better hurt him. They would have her to deal with if they did.

She left the polish rags on the counter and went over to sit by him.

"Need any help, Grandpa?"

"Help?" he asked, not looking up. "A person with no arms or legs needs help. I have both, thank God."

"Just thought I'd ask."

"Thank you just the same."

"Grandpa . . ."

He placed the stamp at the center of the label and pressed down slowly. "Yes?"

"Think you'll be happy here?" She traced the metal edge around the table.

"Why not?"

"Well, I've heard . . . someone told me that North Haven isn't exactly open-minded about things . . . you know, prejudiced sort of."

Still he did not look up. "This is what you heard, eh?"

"Yes. Midge told me."

"Ahhh . . . Midge."

"What's the matter with Midge? She isn't exactly a dummy."

He stamped another label, replaced the stamp to the ink pad and looked up, his eyes meeting hers.

"I don't like that kind of weather forecasting, Deborah," he said softly. "The best way to predict weather is to stick your head out of the window and sniff for yourself."

"And get your ears chopped off in the bargain?" she added.

"Ta, ta, ta." He waved his finger at her. "I've been in more dangerous places than North Haven and I still have my ears. Go sniff for yourself, Deborah, and maybe you'll see that it isn't so cold outside as you thought." He returned to stamping, and she got up.

What was the use of arguing with him about it? Grandpa was like Candide. If you put him through fire and flood, quakes and foils, it was nevertheless the best of all possible worlds. Somehow Grandpa's logic was impenetrable and frustrating, like his reaction to her haircut.

46

The next day Debby stood at the curb in front of the drugstore, waiting. It was the week of North Haven's Village Centennial and a parade was about to begin. She had not wanted to come; but Mother insisted it would be good for her, and Grandpa declared it a perfect opportunity to sniff for herself.

A brass band somewhere was beginning its pum-pum-pum, pumpum-pa and Debby moved in closer. The band was still far off but the excitement was moving steadily up, and suddenly she felt less like a camera—unless, she thought, cameras get pulsy when they click on certain scenes, like parades, like drums, like green banners in the wind.

Cardboard flowerpots dangling yellow and white chrysanthemums were strung on lamp posts, and a giant streamer billowing and shimmering in the sun-tipped wind blared the word CENTENNIAL. Like State Street when the Shriners get it, she thought, then laughed to herself at the absurdity of the comparison. Nothing in the world, let alone the puny prettiness of Lake Road, North Haven, could be compared to State Street when the Shriners got it. The Majestic Department Store flew colored flags, and inside their front show windows a reproduction of North Haven in miniature rested on green felt as though it were a jewel belonging to the store. White houses on broad lawns, big old trees modeled to scale—all were radiating charm and tradition.

Alongside the miniature of modern North Haven was another, the North Haven of one hundred years ago,

47

mostly forest land, a few buildings where the names HAMILTON and RANDALL figured too obviously prominent, the way the names of the pashas would appear in Persia. Just the same, old North Haven was lush with all those trees, and beautiful with Lake Michigan unfurled at its eastern shore like a bolt of aqua silk.

Of the five thousand persons in town, all were out today—a profusion of sun-tanned faces and slick Bermuda shorts. Casual was the word, expensively casual like the pencil-slim figures in *Vogue* gorgeously ruffled. She thought suddenly of Midge and how she would appreciate the fashions here, but she stopped herself. Don't think about Midge, she cautioned. Remain a camera. Cameras have no loyalties, no memories, no feelings.

The band was coming close now; the roll of drums was inside the pit of her stomach despite her resistance, pimpling up her skin, only because they were drums, she thought, not that they belonged to North Haven High students in red and gold capes or to majorettes strutting high in their white boots, breaking the air in swirls of twirling silver. Calm down, she told herself; goose pimples go with loyalties and a sense of belonging, or at least of wanting to belong. It was better to stay a camera. Float after float rolled by and the last one had four young girls sitting at spinning wheels, bringing cheers, whistles, and applause from the crowd. The girl on the top tier of the float was a stunning blonde about her own age. She was dreamy-looking in a pale blue, high-necked dress that fell around her in soft folds from the waist, and she was smiling and waving with poise and grace that Debby had seen only in movies. Here we go again, she thought, *Vogue Magazine* one hundred years back. But the girl on the top tier of the float, calico notwithstanding, was no shrinking lass of another century. Her eyebrow was lifted slightly and there was a proud, unabashed tilt to her chin. A blond, modern Scarlet O'Hara.

Someone spoke close to her ear and she wheeled around, startled, to a tall dark boy who laughed and repeated, "Pat Hamilton up there. Quite a dish, isn't she?"

She found herself answering spontaneously "Yes, isn't she?" without thinking first. This olive-skinned boy resembled Tony so much you had to blink your eyes. Why, if he weren't so close, if you couldn't see details, you might easily take him for Tony. Looking at him gave her a funny, breathless feeling; it made her remember the smoothness of Tony's face against her finger tips, the warmth of his lips when he kissed her at the farewell party. She flushed now, wondering if this lean dark stranger was thinking that his speaking had embarrassed her. If he were thinking it at all, however, he did not let on.

"You've just seen North Haven's aristocracy. Impressed?" he asked.

"Oh, I am." She laughed in spite of herself. There was something about this boy that made ignoring him pointless—the resemblance to Tony perhaps, but more than that. There was nothing contrived in his manner. He seemed free. At second glance, really, he was not like Tony at all. He had the same slim, tall build, perhaps, and lots of thick black hair in need of being cut, but his features were relaxed and not nearly so pronounced as Tony's.

He grinned at her, raising his voice above the Cub Scouts who waved signs that read BE SQUARE and yelped by wildly out of step, ignoring their leaders who were trying to corral them.

"How do you like North Haven?"

"How do you know to ask me that?"

"High-school student, aren't you?"

She nodded.

"Small town. Know all the high-school faces by heart and I haven't seen yours before. What's more," he added, smiling, "don't think I'd miss a face like yours."

She smiled back. Mmmmm, she had almost forgotten how good a compliment like that could feel. But at the same time, she told herself, the handwriting was on the wall. She would be picked out and studied like the Rosetta Stone.

His hands were slung into his blue-jeans pockets. "You haven't answered my question."

"Your question? Oh, yes, North Haven. Ask me next year. I'll be in a better position to say."

"What happens then?"

"The jail sentence ends. I can go where I please."

His eyes widened in puzzlement and she was sorry she had said it. Midge's influence, she told herself, frankness and candor and a full cup of confidence. Coming not from Midge but from her, it sounded loony.

He took his hands out of his pockets and straightened up. "Pretty strong words." Then he smiled again. "Could be an awfully nice jail."

The crowd had thinned around them and the street was disorganized with traffic snarled and with late shoppers making a last dash to groceries, and with overwrought kids being dragged off to automobiles. But the tall boy in the white T shirt seemed in no hurry. She couldn't very well walk away from him, although her mood was far from wanting to make new friends; but there was something about this boy . . . "Well, it's all over now," she said. "The parade, I mean."

"That's what I thought you meant. . . . Say, what's your name? I'm Josh Sandow. Very important family . . . can't understand why we were left out of Majestic's window."

It was hard not to laugh at this Josh Sandow, although he wasn't saying anything hilarious. He had a way, a kind of banter with hooks attached. "Deborah Rose," she answered. "Formerly of Chicago, not important, and Majestic's never gave us a thought."

"Don't let it worry you," he said. "There's the next hundred years to look forward to."

"Will the Sandows make it by then?"

"Couldn't care less." He had his hands in his pockets again and she could hear jingling while he looked suddenly sheepish.

"Had to make sure before I took the plunge," he said.

51

"How about a Coke? New management at the drugstore. Their Cokes won't taste like water for at least another week."

She felt the color rising to her face. Why should she feel suddenly embarrassed about claiming the drugstore as her family's? Never in all her life had she felt that way.

Josh pointed out the new sign; whistled between his teeth, "Rose Pharmacy"; asked if they were related, and when she barely nodded he slapped his head. "Owwww, that crack about the Cokes . . ."

Grandpa was sitting at the table in the back alcove, this time playing chess with himself, beard and skullcap for all of North Haven to see if they explored far enough. Well, she would try it out with Josh, and if he so much as lifted an eyebrow when she said "That's my grandfather. Would you like to meet him?" it would be the end. She would have nothing further to do with him. But Josh only smiled when she took him back.

"I used to play checkers with myself," he told Grandpa. "Figured I was the best player I knew."

"A sensible approach," Grandpa nodded, moving a black rook two spaces up. "Like the old man who was caught talking to himself and explained, "Why shouldn't I? Better to talk with a wise man like myself than to a fool."

She was relieved. Grandpa was making no effort to study Josh. His attention was focused on the chessboard.

Then Mother and Dad came out of the stockroom. They saw Josh, looked at each other silently, communicated the fact that their Debby had found a friend, smiled and came forward as though to a diplomatic reception. Oh, why didn't they stop? He wasn't St. George on the Charger. He was only a boy, someone she had just met. But there they were, beaming sea signals as though they had discovered rare spice in India.

Dad was looking curiously at Josh. "Did you say your name was Sandow? Wonder if it could be the same? I had a good friend, years ago, a medical student who took pharmacology with me. Ernest Sandow, any relation?"

"Yes, sir. That's my Dad's name and he's a doctor."

"Tall, dark hair, glasses?"

"Check."

"Well! What do you think of that? Ernest Sandow after all these years. Terrible how you lose contact with people. Does he practice in North Haven?"

"Not exactly, Mr. Rose. He has an office on Lake Road; but being a surgeon keeps him in Chicago, mostly."

"I see. I see." Dad's face was literally lighted up. "We were hoping for another Jewish family, but to think of Ernest Sandow and his son . . . This calls for a Coke at least. Make one for him, Debby. I have to take Mother with me to sign some papers; we'll be back in, oh, say a half-hour."

He gripped Josh's shoulder, cocked his head, murmured "Ernest Sandow, eh?" and went out with Mother, who was remarking on the smallness of the world and the endless surprises in life.

She went around back of the counter while Josh perched on a stool smiling at her. There was no doubt about it, he was good-looking; even better-looking than Tony, whose tenseness showed too much. It was nice to have the cold, smooth counter, the sound of the fizzing Coke between them so she could stay aloof, keep her hands busy. She pushed the glass toward him.

"Mmmmm," he teased, "that's what I call service."

She was about to bring her own Coke around when the bell on the door jangled and a group of young people came in: three girls and a tall, blond boy, as tall as Josh although he appeared larger somehow. Debby recognized the girl holding on to his arm as the one on the top tier of the float—the stunning one Josh said was Pat Hamilton, quite the dish. They moved closer to the counter, and the blond boy came over to Josh and whacked his shoulder. "New hangout, Joshbo?" He smiled and his clear blue eyes stared directly into hers. She busied herself with tying a tea apron around her waist, hearing his voice drawl, "I can see why, Joshbo. I can see why."

He moved down the counter and plunked on a stool next to Pat Hamilton, who had kept her eyes on his every move and was lowing at him now, "My, my, what big eyes you have."

She was gorgeous, you had to admit it—even more so up close than from the float. If the label "peaches and cream" could be given to anyone, she was entitled to it.

"Would you like something?" Debby asked.

Pat Hamilton said "Oh" as if surprised, as if she saw

54

Debby now for the first time, and replied in a cool voice, "That's right, the McIntyres sold this place, didn't they, and you must be the new . . . new waitress. Cherry Coke please, and heavy on the cherry."

While she winced, Josh called down from the other end of the counter, "Meet Debby Rose, the pharmacist's daughter, first week in North Haven." His voice was deliberate and less casual. "You're a senior, aren't you, Debby?"

She nodded, her face turning warm again, feeling a sense of being framed here with them. There was no exit from this compromising position; no way to hide from the shriveling humiliation of Pat's tasting her Coke, making a face, and then demanding, "More cherry, please."

Steve Randall peered at Debby over the rim of his Coke glass and murmured, "Never you mind. Mine's delicious." She tangled with the hard knot in her throat.

The girl introduced as Mary Carrington chattered to the other one, Angie Kress, a mousy-looking brown-eyed girl with very thick hair. School was starting in two days. They would be back in harness. It was the long last pull. And when did Angie think college counselors would come around? Then she spoke to the boys, not giving Angie a chance to answer her question, glancing first to Steve, then to Josh. "You boys planning on making us famous this year, the basketball pennant for sure?"

The boys looked at each other, exchanging silently a certain knowledge between them—something that had been kept secret until now. Steve swished the Coke in his

55

glass, pensive and hesitant while studying it for a moment, then offhandedly in his same wisecracking manner, said, "You poor little gals. Have to get yourselves another hero."

"What!" Mary shrieked, and Angie sucked her breath in.

"That's the ticket," Steve went on, his nonchalance tottering with nervous laughs. "Bring out the sackcloth—the mighty Casey has struck out."

Pat Hamilton looked as though she'd been hit. "What's the idea?" she said. "You didn't tell me about this."

"Now, beautiful, there are a few things I don't tell you. And what the heck, there's Josh here to carry on."

"Why in the world . . ." Angie mused aloud; and Pat snapped, interrupting her, "Stop being cryptic, Steve; no one goes from being captain to just . . . just nothing."

"Waaaal . . . it's this way," Steve straddled the stool. "Joshbo here plays basketball and studies too . . . old Steve just plays basketball. Get the drift? Want me to spell it out?"

"Those gelatinheads sacked you?" Pat's voice rang with disbelief.

"Look, beautiful, don't make it sound like a personal campaign against Steve Randall . . . a near flunk in chemistry is a near flunk in chemistry, especially if it goes with a near flunk in math and English."

"And old Joshbo here . . ." Pat's face was flushed and her voice sizzled with sarcasm. "Joshbo takes over being captain. Right?" She caught herself, reddened at Angie's little gasp and fleeting glance at Josh. Then she turned back to her Coke glass, sipping at chips of ice at the bottom.

Josh sat there, his face showing no signs of discomposure; but the air radiated tension like heat from a pavement. Glasses pinged against each other as she collected them, and Steve leaned over the counter asking, "New management change the price of Cokes?" She shook her head while he pulled a fifty-cent piece from his pocket and put it down, filling her with panic that the extra dime was for a tip. She swallowed hard, heard the sound of her own voice pitched unfamiliarly high, "Why don't we make it on the house this time? Really, I'm sure Dad won't mind." She pushed the money back toward him, trying to return his smile as he said "Thanks" and pocketed the money.

They started to leave, Mary still chattering about the woes of Monday morning when Angie emitted another one of her little gasps and nudged her, motioning back to the alcove where Grandpa still sat absorbed in his chess game. Pat Hamilton picked up the gesture immediately, then giggled openly. She tugged at Steve's shirt and pointed Grandpa out to him with a quick motion of her head and eyes, then whispered loud enough to be heard at the counter, "North Haven's arrived, hasn't it?"

Steve glanced back at Debby and Josh, his face aglow with embarrassment. He put his hand up, waved a feeble good-by; then the bell over the door jangled, and they were gone.

Josh slipped off the stool and stood a little away from the counter, hesitating as though caught in a storm miles from shelter. He turned slightly toward the door and came back to the counter. When he spoke finally his voice was intimate. "Debby?"

She concentrated on the Coke glasses, which were hard to get clear. Oh, what was the use? It was a frightful encounter, maybe worse for Josh than for her.

"Debby?" She heard him say it again. "There's a Centennial Square Dance tonight. I hadn't planned on going, but . . . Would you like to?"

Grandpa had not heard a thing that witch had said. If she told him, what would he say? Toss it off with an epigram, a wise saying to make everything cozy again? Well, it wasn't enough for her, grass-roots philosophy and a dogged resignation to anything life offered. What was she doing here anyway, googling over a new boy when all she wanted, everything she hoped for, was elsewhere and lost, completely lost.

"I'm sorry, Josh, I can't," she said. "Can I have a rain check?" She undid her apron, smiled back when he said "Sure"; and then the door jangled again—Josh on the other side of it now, standing for a moment at the curb and then walking slowly across Lake Road.

She tossed the apron under the counter; went back to where Grandpa sat and sank into a chair opposite him, barely managing to make a sound when he said, "Beautiful-looking children they were . . . and smart, I can tell."

How can I get out of this? she asked herself. What do you do about things? She had put her head out of the window. She had sniffed for herself.

Five

~~~~~~

"Just because . . ." she answered while rinsing her toothbrush, aware of Mother leaning against the frame of the bathroom door, watching her.

"That's no answer," Mother replied. "Don't you want to look nice?"

"Not particularly."

Mrs. Rose followed her into the bedroom and closed the door. It was not so easy as all that to dismiss Mother, and something more than banter was in the atmosphere now.

"You're the one," she said, "who requires two hours' solitude in the bathroom to wash your hair."

"But things have changed," Debby answered in a sing-song, yanking at a strand of her short hair and clinging to a pose of aloofness that was rapidly disintegrating. She wished Mother would leave her alone, give her time to answer her own questions about why it seemed important not to dress up this first morning of school. Oh, but the answer was simple once you really faced it. For whom? For what? It was all right to look neat; the green skirt and a white blouse would do. But if you took special pains after clapping it into your head that you didn't care about making an impression, wasn't it kidding yourself; wasn't it outright hypocrisy? And suppose you did dress up and still got ignored? Oh, no! The green gabardine could weather a snubbing, but not the beige.

Mother said "Deborah" in a tone that portended a final offensive. "Your attitude is what's wrong. You're doing everything you can to make Dad and me feel guilty."

For a moment Debby was thrown off course. Did they really feel guilty? Good. That was satisfying—like having said you'll be sorry, and being alive to see it. Yet, after the initial sweetness of revenge? She gave in, wore the new beige skirt and left the house with the conviction that at least she'd look nice when she was thrown to the lions.

As she came closer to the school, she could see crowds of students already gathered at the front entrance of the low rambling building. She had thought she would arrive earlier than they; that she could avoid mingling through the groups she had imagined laughing and chattering about their summer activities just as she had done at Purcell. But she had not come early enough; the entire student body, or so it appeared, was already there.

Two diagonal walks on a broad lawn led up to the front entrance and both were a blur of faces and voices, color and sound, which she inched around carefully, trying not to brush up against anyone. Someone moved backward out of a circle and a great push practically knocked her over. She blinked for a moment and then recognized Steve Randall, the boy in the drugstore that awful afternoon. While he apologized she flushed with embarrassment, remembering the first meeting that was still too fresh for comfort. He looked at her with the same half-joking, half-serious interest he had shown then.

"It's you," he said. "The Coke maker. The beautiful Coke maker." His eyes were very blue against his tan, and his teasing smile was unmistakably good-natured.

"Hi," she answered, looking beyond him now at Pat Hamilton, who stood just an arm's length from Steve, poised and sleekly attractive, watching him. She made no move to come closer or to greet her in any way. Steve noticed too, and frowned a little; then he apologized again, adding with a chuckle that not everyone at North Haven was as clumsy as he. She smiled once more, and turned quickly inside.

The smell of the building was cool and clean; no pine-oil fragrance here to give assurance of its having been scrubbed, but an uncorrupted freshness that accompanies new things. She moved farther into the foyer to take her first look at North Haven High. It was a maze of terrazzo floors and airy corridors, stairways and fluorescent lights, and historical wall murals of Illinois and Lincoln.

"*All* the way from the South Side, Deborah?" Miss Lipton, her home-room teacher, said it, Debby thought, as though it had meant crossing the Himalayas.

Cheerfully then, almost as though she were grateful

61

for the opportunity, Miss Lipton introduced her to Elly Freed, a tall, dark-haired girl with large brown eyes that looked slightly surprised. She was cemented to Elly right off, out of thoughtfulness no doubt. (You had to believe that, didn't you?) Yet, when Elly's saccharine sweetness was too much, it was hard not to credit Miss Lipton with the irritating supposition that she and Elly would have loads in common. She could have introduced her first to anyone; to the crisp-looking girl in the back row, or the blond one with the red wool skirt who had smiled so readily. But Miss Lipton had blended her and Elly like the ingredients for instant coffee, and the mixture was supposedly reliable.

Elly Freed tacitly made the same assumption. She eyed Debby sympathetically. "I hear it's worth your life, your actual life, to go out at night on the South Side." Elly inflected the word "life" and her eyes grew wide; but before Debby could answer, Elly galloped ahead, "It's different here, a higher-class neighborhood and all—oh, but I didn't mean . . . My, what a good-looking skirt, Debby! And you will eat with us in the lunchroom, won't you? There will be six of us now."

This last announcement in Elly's rapid monologue made her start. "What do you mean, six of us now?" she asked, suspecting all too keenly what Elly meant, yet reluctant to accept the conclusion.

Elly's wide eyes grew even wider, but she lowered her voice. "My goodness, maybe I've . . . But you *are* Jewish, aren't you?" Debby nodded, and Elly's expression relaxed. "Six Jewish girls," she explained. "Senior girls, that is. There are quite a few in the junior class, but there were just five of us in the senior class. We have lunch together."

"Oh. Thanks for the invitation, Elly . . . nice of you."

Elly was nice all that morning. She helped Debby from class to class, introduced her to teachers, helped her find a seat—in short, took over. Debby saw North Haven High School through Elly's wide eyes and she began to feel as though being a friend of Elly's was like snuggling up to the oracle. "Don't ever forget your gym suit," Elly said, "because of the demerits," and, another time, in a breathless tone she announced, "Wait until you see Mr. Gastrey—oh, just wait—he's divine."

She's like Andrea, Debby thought, and followed Elly into the lunch-room din with impunity.

Elly brought her to the table of the five as though she were a trophy.

"Deborah Rose," she announced, and then pointed out Sally, Jean, Myra, Pam, and Sue.

"How do you like it here?" Jean asked directly. She was the tallest girl Debby had ever seen; if she judged correctly, Jean was at least five feet ten inches. The girl sitting next to her, Sue, was a tiny thing, dark hair that curled all over her head in Italian style, a small upturned nose, and eyes that sparkled in brown lights. The two girls against the background of the crowded lunch room, the noise, and the moving about had the effect of

63

an Alice in Wonderland—too tiny and too tall, and all confusion.

"It's—it's fine," she said. "A little confusing on the first day."

"It'll stay that way for a while," Jean answered, digging into a plate of macaroni and cheese, "and after that," she continued with a full mouth, "it gets bewildering. Take Long Jean's word for it."

The girls laughed, but Debby couldn't—not yet, anyway. She felt sorry that Jean had referred to herself in that way because she was now Long Jean forever, and had not given herself a chance to be anything else.

The girls talked among themselves and she was content to listen passively until Sue mentioned Steve Randall's name, calling him the dreamiest guy at North Haven; then she found herself paying full attention.

For the few minutes after lunch Elly took her to a part of the building she had not yet seen, a wing devoted to painting and music. There were several large art rooms with easels standing about, half-rolled canvases on countertops—a casually disheveled room filled with the pungent odors of paint and turpentine. Farther down the hall was the music department and, as they walked past, Debby heard the sounds of a piano behind a closed door. Someone was trying to play a Schubert sonata and was making a terrible mess of it. She had the sudden impulse to open the door, see who was playing; but she held back, clenching her hands instead.

"Anything wrong?" Elly asked, eying her curiously.

"No, of course not," she answered, and stepped up her walk to keep pace with Elly, who had suddenly begun to rush.

The rest of the afternoon went by swiftly and at three-thirty she saw Josh for the first time all day.

"Hi!" he said, catching up with her outside Miss Lipton's room. A gray sweat shirt hung loosely from his slim shoulders, and his black hair was wet and combed back softly as though he had just come from the shower room.

"How did it go today?" he asked. "I see you got the doll for home room."

Debby smiled at him and together they walked to her locker. "She's nice, even sort of sweet."

"All smiles you mean?" Josh feigned a sigh. "Though life will rankle and worlds will crack, Miss Lipton's smile forever stays—"

Debby laughed. "Like the cat in *Alice?*"

"Like the cat in *Alice*."

"But she does have nice teeth."

"Oh, but she smokes."

"My goodness, Josh, how do you know that?"

"Common knowledge," Josh answered nonchalantly. "She runs to the faculty lounge twenty times a day for a smoke."

Debby laughed in earnest, imagining tiny, white-haired Miss Lipton with her cheeks puffed up, dragging madly at a cigarette in the faculty lounge.

"She doesn't impress me as a derelict exactly."

65

"Now, now, now. Don't let appearances fool you, don't stereotype; it's like saying you can tell the face of a criminal."

Debby took two books from her locker and turned to face Josh again. "Listen," she said, still chuckling, "I merely said—"

"Shall I walk you home?" he asked. "Haven't had a merit badge in ages."

"Sure," Debby answered. "But I wish you hadn't compared Miss Lipton to telling the face of a criminal. It unsettles me somehow." They both laughed again.

Josh took her home a longer way, around the back of the school and over two blocks where the lake front stretched beyond Frontage Boulevard, a beautiful wide street of lovely old homes and towering trees on one side, a park on the other with steps leading down to the beach. They walked along the park side for a while, Josh's hands slung deep in his pants pockets, his hair mostly dried now and curling softly about his forehead. Their flip mood had turned to a quieter tone that seemed to go with the old trees of the park.

"Like it here?" Josh asked.

"Beautiful," Debby answered, bending down to pick up a twig from the grass. "Lovely . . . the trees are so full—"

"That's not what I mean."

She picked the bark from her twig, concentrating on it while she answered. "I don't know yet, Josh. That's something I don't want to talk about—ever." She changed the subject before he could probe any further. "How did the basketball business work out? Are you captain?"

"Yep," he said, "and headed for glory."

She hesitated. "I'll bet that really rankles some people around here."

Josh looked surprised. "My being captain rankles? Why?"

"I just thought—well . . . it's true, isn't it, that Steve Randall is a kind of patriotism around North Haven—to say nothing of that Hamilton girl."

"Say," Josh said, looking surprised, "What have you got against Steve Randall?"

She had not expected this reaction from him; to her, the situation was obvious and had not escaped anyone, least of all Josh, who had been the butt of Pat Hamilton's snide remarks.

"But the way Pat Hamilton sniped at you . . ."

They had crossed over from the park now, headed west toward her house. Josh swung his arm around her shoulder and said casually, "She'll get over it. What there is between me and the team, Pat Hamilton could never know about."

Debby walked beside him silently, wondering how he came by his abundant self-confidence. She'll get over it, he says. Just like that. Such neat assurance; neat and nice and normal. Tony, for example, would have blown up, hashed things out, demanded justice, but not Josh; he was calm; he was unruffled, safe and sound and stable.

Her house was in sight now, and Josh slowed his walk.

"Say," he said, "how would you like to go bowling Saturday night?"

She snapped herself back. "Oh, swell. I'd love that."

"Or maybe you'd rather do something else? A concert? Any burning interests?"

She felt her face flush as she found herself reacting to the word "concert." What if she said she *did* want to go to a concert? Would it lead to his wanting to talk about music, and then herself getting caught up and maybe blurting everything out?

"No," she answered. "No burning interests. Bowling is just my speed."

Six

Deborah made friends in spite of herself. The smiling blond girl in her home room turned out to be Madie Weeks, and the second week of school, after Elly relaxed her hold, she and Madie sought each other more and more.

Madie was a lively, vivacious girl with a snappy walk and a way of smiling at you with forthright honesty. The two girls laughed a lot together and Debby teased Madie about frittering her time away on school committees, but she grew to admire Madie's way of finding fun and interest in everything. It was through Madie that Debby found herself getting involved, too. At first Madie would ask simply, "Please help me with sending out notices for the Dramatics Club rehearsals," or, "Can you come over tonight and help me get the lists straightened out for the Social Committee?" And then, finally, she came right out and said that no one, absolutely no one, had volunteered to work on decorations for the informal senior dance.

"Okay," Debby sighed. "You hooked me."

Madie virtually pounced on her. "You'll never regret it, my friend; you'll thank me, you'll be eternally grateful."

"When do we start?" Debby asked. "Remember, I'm doing it only because you seem to be stuck."

"Oh, I'm not exactly stuck. The dance isn't for almost two months yet."

"Why, Madie Weeks! You trapped me."

Madie did not answer, but tossed her head back and smiled in her special way.

For the next six weeks North Haven bathed in Indian summer. September, then October sifted through a golden autumn sieve of burnished colors in the yard, leaves blown gently into piles under the spiraea bushes, a final blooming of the roses too perfect to dwell upon except for the contrast of sturdy mum stalks budding yellow and orange and purple. The maple tree blazed above Debby's bedroom window and all of North Haven was a palette of mixed colors against white frame and stucco houses with ivy vines twisting aimlessly around chimneys and down to window frames. Elm Street, where they lived, was especially lovely with its giant Dutch elms stanchly implanted on the parkways like sentinels against bleak intrusion from the city.

The weather was becoming crisp now, but every morning without fail Grandpa was out in the back yard digging up tulip bulbs, clipping bushes and preparing them for the following spring. Debby had watched him through her bedroom window from time to time, but this morning, early in November, she stepped around to the back of the house before breakfast.

Grandpa was digging around the bushes on his hands and knees. She stood there for a moment watching him as he bent over, his aged body frail and thin even with the bulky sweater he wore to pad him; his white hair and beard catching the still pale sunlight, but the rest of his sharp, protruding features shaded and shadowy. He had changed since coming here, Debby thought. When they lived in the city he seemed exclusively devoted to chess, books, and conversation; but now he had returned to working in the soil by the hour, digging on his hands and knees as though he believed in it beyond anything else. She wondered if all old people, after a lifetime, return to the pleasures of their childhood, and she remembered Grandpa's telling her about his father's garden in Poland and his mouth-watering descriptions of succulent giant strawberries plucked from their beds and eaten unwashed by the dozen.

Grandpa noticed her standing there and he called to her as he rose laboriously to his feet.

"Come see the mums," he said.

She went to the edge of the lawn where a border of purple mums had bloomed only a few days ago.

"They're pretty," she said.

"Why don't you pick some?" Grandpa asked. "It is good to get acquainted with living things."

"I'm not used to them, I guess. They look painted instead of real."

Grandpa clucked his tongue. "A city girl, eh? And

flowers are for picture books? Here—pick some; see how real they are."

She squatted near the tall stalks of the mums, sniffed and inhaled a pungence that had no real odor. When she touched the coarse edges of the flower, delicately tracing the scalloped edges with her finger, Grandpa chuckled. "Well, city girl?" he said. "Are they painted or real?"

She laughed, reached for the clippers and began to cut them—carefully at first, timidly, as though exploring a new acquaintance; uncertain, still afraid to take liberties, but Grandpa enthusiastically declared that she had the air of a real gardener.

When she had cut enough for a bouquet she handed the clippers back to him. "Thanks for the initiation, Grandpa, but I'd better get some breakfast—"

"Wait a minute, Debby," he said, coming closer to her. "How is it in school now, my child?"

"Oh. Not as bad as I had thought. I'm on a committee. There's going to be a dance and I'm making decorations. I'm an artist! Imagine that!"

"Good. Good," Grandpa said. "I hope you'll have more courage with that than you have with the piano."

"Let's not go into that again."

"I'm not going into anything—I just want to tell you that your mother in there still washes the piano keys with milk every Friday."

"So? That's nothing new," she answered.

"It's a waste," Grandpa said flatly. "Children are starving in the world, so why should your idle piano drink milk?"

She shook her head at him. "No you don't, Grandpa. The starving children will get you nowhere this time; anyway it's Mother that's wasting the milk, not me." She kissed him quickly on the cheek, gathered the mums in her arms, and went into the house for breakfast.

When she entered her home room that morning Miss Lipton handed her a note from Mr. Stewart, head of North Haven's Music Department, with permission to see him during study hour. All that morning she could only stare at things, thinking of her meeting with Mr. Stewart, wondering what he wanted with her. In biology class she jumped a foot, thinking she had seen a dead frog move his leg; in English she had answered that *For Whom the Bell Tolls* was written by John Donne, the title taken from a poem by Ernest Hemingway. Even when Miss Fucella corrected her in a surprised tone of voice, saying it was the other way around, she only nodded, the information not really registering.

When the time came, finally, for her meeting with Mr. Stewart, she made her way to the arts wing of the school deeply engrossed in herself, not looking where she was going, and before she could stop she collided with a large form coming out of the art studio. She looked up and gasped.

"Oh! Not again! I'm so sorry."

Steve Randall's blue eyes smiled down at her and his hands firmly gripped her shoulders. She felt her heart give a peculiar thump, even more pronounced than the first time she had had a sudden close contact with him. She stepped back quickly, apologizing again.

"Say," he said. "Think these collisions mean anything? You know, like we're prone to each other?"

She stood away from him, latching onto a paper that protruded from her notebook, straightening it meticulously while she controlled her fingers.

"Oh, no," she said, and then she was stuck for words. Steve was looking at her intently and she felt her whole body tingling.

"I like the way you play tennis," he said.

"Tennis?" she repeated, confused.

"Yes," he laughed. "I watched you on the courts the other day; nice swing—nice shorts, too."

She felt her face turn warm and she could mutter an only half-coherent "Thank you."

"I've seen you in the lunch room, too."

"Oh, yes," she mumbled, and hoped fervently that he had not noticed her staring at him. She had promised herself a thousand times not to look where he sat with three other boys, Pat Hamilton, and the pinched-looking Angie Kress.

But her promises were becoming an artless game without rules. Steve pulled her eyes in his direction, the large contours of his build compelling her to watch for his expressions, to steal glimpses of him running his hands through his thick, blond hair. They had caught each other once—no, many times—in a fleeting exchange of glances, like wild deer in a forest, and always she had turned quickly from his steady blue eyes, avoiding his half-smile. Then she would promise herself that she would either stop or go somewhere else to eat.

For over a month now she and Steve Randall had been watching each other, stealing glances, waiting, and now for the second time she had fallen into his arms.

He smiled at her again, a slow, lingering smile. "Sure no bones are broken?" he asked finally.

"Oh, no," she answered. "I'm fine." Silently though, she racked herself. Why can't I say something more intelligent than "Oh, yes" and "Oh, no?" Why? Why?

They stood there for a moment longer, said good-by; then Debby stepped quickly, almost running to Mr. Stewart's room.

"Miss Rose?" he asked. His whole manner said "No familiarity"—not at all like a musician, Debby thought. He looked like an insurance salesman, neat horn-rimmed glasses, balding head, an immaculate gray suit with all the buttons fastened on the jacket, and a round, darkish mole at the side of his nose. How different he was from Mr. Mason! The thought of Mr. Mason was a claw inside her and the prissy-looking man before her underscored her longing to be back with her old teacher. She could not imagine music beneath this Mr. Stewart's neatly buttoned jacket, nor passion behind his thick horn-rimmed glasses.

His tone was businesslike when he repeated, "Miss Rose, I have a letter here from Donald Mason, a former teacher of yours."

There was a catch in her throat at the realization that

Mr. Mason had written, and that she was now redis-
covered. It was like an avalanche of happiness; it was
like waking up and finding herself back in the old apartment; it was like putting her hand to her hair that was
soft and long again; it was like looking forward to the
Purcell music competition.

Mr. Stewart waved to a chair and spoke again; this
time his voice had more warmth.

"You haven't played at all since coming to North
Haven, have you, Miss Rose?"

Goodness, she thought, he's clairvoyant on top of it all.
"No, sir," she answered. "I haven't." (She marveled at
herself calling him "sir.")

"Mr. Mason seems to think you have extraordinary
talent. He also said you had quite a disappointment."

"Yes, sir. I did. It was terrible . . . I . . ." She
wanted all at once to tell him everything, because only
a musician would understand what she had been through
—the pain, the longing, the holding back—but in a
glance she caught the cool detachment of his face and
said simply, looking down at her fingernails, "It was very
disappointing."

"Well," Mr. Stewart said matter-of-factly while getting up from his desk, "all artists have disappointments.
Some are worse than others, but they all have them. The
important thing is to start over. How do you feel about
that?"

"I had decided not to, Mr. Stewart. I told Mr.
Mason—"

"Oh?" His eyebrows crept over the rim of his glasses. "Well, you see—"

"Miss Rose," he interrupted her, "would you play something for me?"

He went to the piano and thumbed through some music lying on top—and before she had a chance to say yes or no, he was holding out a book of Beethoven sonatas. "Know any of these?" he asked. "Or, better still, play anything you like. Mr. Mason says you're good with Chopin."

She went to the piano bench and sat down. Trembling, she removed the ring from her right hand and placed it on top of the piano, flexing her fingers as she pulled it off. She adjusted herself to the bench and took a deep breath, placing her fingers on the keys for the opening bars of the Chopin ballade. Then, for the first time in almost two months, she was playing again and it was a thrilling, giddy sensation, like being at the top of a Ferris wheel, swinging there with the dark starlit sky all around her.

But after a few minutes of playing, the Ferris wheel came down with a bump and the stiffness in her fingers turned to clumsiness, and the muscles of her hands and upper arms pained from lack of use and practice. It would be later, when her fingers had to move rapidly and precisely, that the clammy stiffness might stop her altogether, but she tried, for now, to at least establish the mood of the piece: a green field at twilight . . . lovers in a green field . . . Steve asking her if they were prone to each other . . . prone to each other . . . lovers at dusk. . . . The tempo wasn't right somehow . . . there, that was better when the key changed. A few more bars of largo; but it was wrong, all wrong.

She stopped in the middle of a measure when a shooting pain went through her knuckles. She knew she could not relax her fingers even if she tried, and she dropped them in her lap in a gesture of hopelessness. When she looked up to Mr. Stewart's thick glasses they seemed to swim elusively before her eyes. "I'm sorry," she said. "I'm out of practice, I guess."

"Yes, quite likely," he answered. "But I've taken that into consideration, and even so, Miss Rose, I frankly think you would have had to do much better than that to win the Purcell competition."

The words hit her like a shower of ice, freezing her to the piano bench.

"Miss Rose," he continued, "your technique would hardly get you through a concerto. If I were you, I'd go back to exercises. Simple Bach. You do show promise, but right at the moment you're all cramped and tense and not good—not good at all. Exercises are your answer, not concertos."

She felt a tightening of her face, and her eyes squinted at him of their own accord. Who did he think he was? What right had he to draw these conclusions after hearing only part of a score? She hadn't even finished and the ballade was something she knew well, even if she had shown some nervousness. What a highhanded, tactless

man he was! Mr. Mason raved about her Chopin, and this
. . . this undertaker said she played badly and wouldn't
have won the scholarship anyway.

When he spoke again his voice was lifeless, monotonous, and yet there was a quality in it she could not ig-
nore.

"I hope you can take criticism, Miss Rose. If you work
with me you'll get plenty of it."

She didn't answer. Work with him? That would be the
day of miracles; she wasn't crazy yet. She managed to
sit up straight and take another long look at him; the
top button on his neat gray jacket was undone now. He
must have unbuttoned it while she was playing.

"I don't believe I'll go back to music," she said, and
the defiance in her own voice surprised her.

"That's up to you," he answered. "No one can talk an
artist into being one. It's just there. Did you know, Miss
Rose, that Northwestern gives music scholarships?"

"No, sir. I didn't."

He walked back to his desk and started sorting papers.
It was a gesture of dismissal and she got up from the
piano bench, starting toward the door. He held his hand
up to stop her and, still not looking up from his papers,
he added his final words.

"I didn't say you could win one, mind you. Your technique is pretty sloppy . . . but it might be worth a try.
See what you can do with these exercises." He held out
a book of Bach piano pieces.

As she went to take them, he looked her full in the face

79

for the first time. "You know, Miss Rose," he said, "Chopin has a way of making the head swim, and I think you might do with some sobering up."

She stood there listening, clutching the book of music tightly in her hands, shouting silently back at him—the nerve, the gall, the undiluted gall; twenty bars of music and he had the nerve to make such judgments.

She murmured a half-coherent "Thank you" and left the room.

Seven

"Great Scott! Did we go into the catering business?" Debby asked.

The kitchen counter was strewn with canisters, baking tins, ladles, open packages of ground nuts and raisins, bowls of soft bread crumbs and minced celery. Mrs. Rose had a full apron on and a blue bandanna around her hair as she did on let's-dig-into-the-house days. She hardly looked up from mixing batter when Debby came into the kitchen.

"Expecting the King of France?" Debby asked once more, popping a handful of nuts into her mouth.

"Don't eat the nuts," Mrs. Rose answered. "Help if you want to, but don't pick."

"Why all the stuff? Thanksgiving isn't for two weeks yet."

Mrs. Rose looked puzzled, then smiled. "I forgot, dear," she said. "You were in school when the letter came. He's coming home tomorrow for the week end."

"Who? Mark?" She felt a quick exhilaration.

"Certainly Mark." Mrs. Rose stopped mixing. "Anyone else you know could be coming for the week end?"

"Nope. Not a breathing soul, but I'm glad about Mark coming tomorrow. I have a movie date with Josh tonight."

"My," Mrs. Rose answered, pulling the dish of nuts close to where she worked, "you've been seeing quite a bit of Josh, haven't you? That's nice; he's a lovely boy. . . . Debby, please stay away from the nuts; get yourself an apple and come peel these potatoes."

"Potato kugel, I'll bet," she said, and leaned against the refrigerator door peering in at the assortment of bottles, plastic dishes of leftovers, and packages neatly wrapped in tin foil. The bottom shelf had been removed and in its place was a dressed turkey, its legs unbound so it seemed to be lying on its back and scratching at the shelf above. Sheer cannibalism, she thought.

"Yes, m'girl, potato kugel," Mrs. Rose answered with a touch of defiance. "We haven't had it for ages—not since Mark was home last, six months ago."

"Fattening," Debby said flatly. "A thousand calories to the half-morsel," and then, taking the potato peeler from Mother, she asked, "Is Mark coming home for something special, or just coming home?"

"He says he has news."

"Maybe he won a jingle contest again. Remember the last one?" She raised her arm and recited:

"Some soaps try to sterilize,
Some soaps try to polish,
But, friends, remember Chixo Soap
If you want dirt demolished."

She brought the potato peeler over her heart and bowed. "Courtesy of Mark Rose and Igor Stanislavsky. Or was it Boris? Mischa?"

"Silly," Mrs. Rose answered. "Dad and I figured it all out. This is the time for acceptances to medical school. What else could it be?"

Debby dug into the eye of a potato. "Mark doesn't want to go to medical school," she blurted out, knowing that she was treading deep water, yet unable to curb an impulse to uncover the old and battered truth—the truth about Mark's never having wanted to go to medical school that Dad slid over with backslapping reassurances that sounded like the college rooting section.

Mrs. Rose, however, ignored Debby's remark, pretending with an obvious shrug and batting of eyes not to have heard. "Wouldn't it be wonderful if Mark were to go to Northwestern Medical School, only an hour and a half from home?" And then she worried aloud about the grind affecting his health.

Debby did not answer; she worked at peeling the potatoes, resolved not to stir up any more controversy. There was no doubt about it, she thought; at this moment, as far as her parents were concerned, Mark Rose was the lofty Arrowsmith to whom Mother had given birth and whom Dad had nurtured with a homespun yet elevating philosophy. She wondered if this was the rubber stamp of parenthood: Mother plying with food and anxiety, Father with wisdom and certainty. When she had children, she wanted to be something more; she wanted . . . Oh, who knew what she wanted? She was peeling half the potato away.

"Finished, dear?" Mrs. Rose asked, tossing her wooden mixing ladles to the side of the sink. "If not, I'll take over. Will you give Mark's room a dusting? Air it out a little?"

"Anything you say," she said, relinquishing the peeler. "After all, we're preparing for royalty . . . perhaps you would like his floor scrubbed, the windows washed, and a quick coat of paint on the walls?"

"No," Mrs. Rose said, ignoring her, "I don't think so. Dusting is all . . ."

Mark had been given the large attic room because it was cozy up there and because, Mother said, he was old enough to want complete privacy. When, oh, when, she thought, according to Mother's formula was the age of wanting complete privacy? Grandpa was too old to need it; she was not old enough; Mother and Dad didn't feel entitled to it; but Mark was of the proper age somehow, crucial, as though he were about to enter a human derby and needed a time of quiet reflection beforehand.

Mother had moved all of his stuff up here into the attic, things he probably didn't remember he had, like old baseball mitts, football shoulder guards, a fossil collection, a junior microscope set, and two pairs of ice skates. They lay in a corner neatly boxed and she wondered if they were kept there for any reason other than Mother's reluctance to throw things away. Perhaps they were meant to round out the atmosphere of quiet reflection; but one thing was certain, she was not going to dust them.

She spent more time with the books than she had planned, opening some of them at random: a volume of Proust she remembered Mark calling a bargain at seventy-five cents; a battered copy of Homer in Greek, although she was sure Mark could not read Greek; a beat-up edition of Karl Marx's essays that Mother declared ridiculous no matter how little he paid for it.

By the time she had finished flipping through the pages, she was certain that Mark's news was not his acceptance by a medical school. What was it then? She felt a surge of impatience to see him, to talk to him. She had been saving it all up; suppressing the impulse once or twice to write, because it seemed unnatural somehow and he would not have answered anyway. Their relationship had progressed from teasing and quarreling to tolerance . . . and then, last spring, to a sort of closeness. Well, he would be here tomorrow and she would tell him that she understood the things he had said then about the world being muddled, about his searching, about trying to untangle the crossed wires inside himself. She understood him now—too well—but then, she had only been able to pretend and wonder.

She gave a final wisk of the dustcloth to Mark's bureau and went downstairs to a pickup dinner of salad and cold cuts. Tomorrow they would feast; the maestro would be home to sniff the orchestrated aromas of kugel and two honey cakes and a turkey roasting in the oven.

The movie turned out to be a bad one and Josh whispered to her in the theater that he was willing to leave *if* she was.

"Can't stand leaving anything in the middle," she whispered back. "Anyway I'm dying to see who gets the girl."

"You *know*, don't you?"

"Nope."

Josh groaned, and the people sitting in back coughed and muttered something about noise.

Debby giggled quietly as Josh slumped deep into his seat and stared at the screen.

When it was over, finally, and they were walking down Lake Street, Josh took her hand. "Well? Were you surprised?"

"Surprised at what?"

"At who got the girl?"

She laughed. "Oh, sure, everything surprises me. I'm the dumb type."

"That's what I figured," Josh answered. "What about me? Do I surprise you?"

"What do you mean?"

"We've been to a lot of movies together, eaten a couple dozen hamburgers between us; our families have had dinner together and I—Well, I've been such a good boy."

She did not answer immediately. She and Josh had had a lot of fun together. She liked him; but how much, she didn't know. He still reminded her of Tony and she felt a certain excitement at the first glimpse of him every time, but after they were together the excitement dissolved into a kind of game that was friendly, chatty, and joking. When he held her hand it felt warm and comfortable, too comfortable perhaps, not the way it was with Tony who had a way of making you fidget just by looking at you, but maybe that was childish; maybe the way she felt about Josh was how it was when you got older.

"You don't surprise me," she said finally. "We're—uh, platonic, aren't we?"

"Maybe you are," he answered.

"Gee, it's almost eleven o'clock," she remarked, and felt stupid.

"Don't change the subject, Debby."

"I don't know what to say . . . honestly I like you a lot, Josh."

"Okay," he answered. "Let's have a Coke."

Afterward, at the door of her house, she let him kiss her and his lips on hers felt warm and comfortable and she felt content inside and wondered if this, after all, was love.

She switched the light on in the hall, heard someone say "Hi!" and, after emitting a startled gasp, saw Mark coming toward her.

87

He lifted her off her feet and swung her around, while she could only cackle at him, "I thought you were coming tomorrow!"

"As you see, I'm here tonight—in the flesh. Say! What did you do to your hair?"

Her hand shot up. She had become accustomed to short hair now, three months after cutting, and she took it for granted, even liked the way it curled softly around her face.

She laughed. "Oh, that. Very complicated. I began growing and the hair wouldn't go along, and I became bigger than the hair, and now . . . well, I'm out of proportion, I suppose."

Mark listened, smiling at her. He looked wonderful. His shock of reddish brown hair seemed casually superior to comb and brush, his blue eyes were piercingly alive and vibrant even behind the black-rimmed glasses, and his broad smile revealed white, even teeth.

Mark narrowed his eyes and held her at arm's length. "Hmmmm," he said, "I'd say your proportions have improved considerably since last spring. Why, girl, you almost look human!"

They went into the living room and she sank down on the sofa beside him. "Where is everyone? Don't tell me they walked out on the King of France!"

"Nope. They just went to bed. I gave them a bad time."

She looked at him curiously, but said nothing, while Mark seemed suddenly engrossed in studying the living room.

"Where'd we get that?" he asked, pointing to an old brown leather sofa in the corner.

She groaned. "The old owners left it, didn't even bother to move it. But you know Mother; she's not exactly the type to throw things away, so we all have to act as though it were bequeathed." Mark laughed. "How do you like living in a house? Still a city cliff dweller at heart? I was afraid I'd find you in pigtails and gingham."

"Don't worry," she said. "The only pigtails around here are in the Chinese laundry. As for gingham . . ."

Mark whistled softly. "I detect a dash of bitters, m'girl."

"Do you? Well . . ."

He glanced at her obliquely. "Had a fight with the boy friend tonight? I hear you're rousting about with a fine upstanding lad that's on his way to medical school."

"Holy Moses! How things get blown up around here! He's only a friend. Now listen, brother," she said, pulling on his sleeve. "Come out with it. I'll bet *you're* not going to med school."

Mark's eyes widened at her. "How'd you guess? You're right, but that's not all." He reached inside his jacket and pulled out a photograph. "Stella," he said, and Debby breathed "Wow!"

The girl in the photograph had an olive, Mediterranean complexion and long black hair parted neatly in the middle with a narrow green ribbon holding it back from her face. Her eyes were wide and as black as her hair, and her full red mouth only suggested a smile. She was not beautiful, but her features were strangely engrossing,

89

magnetic almost, not the sort of face you saw often.

He hesitated while he took the picture from her and then got up from the sofa and stood near the window, lighting a cigarette. He inhaled deeply, blew the smoke out, and said, "Dad and Mother are fit to be tied. I'm too young, still wet behind the ears as our father lovingly put it, wrecking my career, et cetera, et cetera, but I'm going to marry her. Very soon."

"Wow!" she repeated. "No wonder they went to bed. They must have flipped. You told them about her—uh, Stella—the same time you told them about medical school?"

"Of course. Poor Dad. He just can't believe I'm not giving up med school because of Stella. He can't understand I don't want to be a doctor—oh, yes, he flipped all right!"

"Wow!"

"Stop saying 'Wow.' I'm not a trapeze act. I'm getting married."

"Oh, Mark, I'm sorry. She—Stella—is gorgeous, like an —an Oriental, or something." She felt her face turn warm. She wanted to be demonstrative, say "Congratulations" with a boom in her voice, but she couldn't. She was not comfortable in sharing big things with Mark, and the photograph of this dark, mysterious girl had taken her by surprise. "Is she, uh, Persian?" she managed to eke out.

Mark threw his head back and laughed. There! She had said the wrong thing again. She would never catch up with Mark. He was always miles ahead of her in a world she knew nothing about. He put his hand on her shoulder. "No," he said. "She's not Persian. Hungarian. And 'Wow' all you like. That's the way I feel about Stella, too."

"I'm glad, Mark." She was on the verge of tears. "But what will you *do*? I mean if you don't go to medical school?"

"I'm going to be a writer."

"A writer?"

"You sound like Dad," Mark said, laughing again. "When I told him, he repeated it as though I had said elephant trainer or organ grinder. Don't worry. I have a job promised on a newspaper when I graduate—we won't become burdens."

"Do you think they'll ever resign themselves to it?"

"Journalism or Stella?"

"Both, I guess."

"I think so, peanut. But it won't be easy for Dad—he had a lot of dreams pinned on me. Did you know he wanted to be a doctor when he was young, but couldn't because of money?"

"He did? Gee, I never thought he wanted anything but that store."

"He wanted a lot more, I guess, but I can't live his lost ambitions—I have some of my own to take care of."

"You want to be a writer terribly, Mark?"

"Yes," he answered softly. "Terribly! Nothing can stop me."

She looked away from him. Once she had wanted something terribly and now it was as though it never existed. How did Mark have the strength to go after what he wanted no matter what Dad thought and said? He wasn't always this confident and certain. But how had he changed? What had made the difference?

Mark looked at her questioningly. "Why all the ponderous silences, Deb . . . the heavy brood stuff?"

"Just thinking about something . . . last spring, for instance. You were different and you said you thought the world was muddled, and I couldn't understand when you talked to me about it."

Mark scratched behind his ear. "Last spring?"

"Don't you remember? About the confusion and everything?"

"I talked to *you* about that?"

She looked away from him. "I wasn't much help, but . . ."

"I'm sorry, peanut. I didn't mean it that way, but honestly I can't remember. So much has happened since then."

"And you've untangled the crossed wires inside yourself?"

"Crossed wires! Did I flip, or what?" He came back to the sofa and sat down beside her. "What's wrong, Deb? Is it your music?"

She did not answer, and she was conscious of his watching her while she slowly pulled a thread from the seam of her skirt and wound it around her finger.

"It'll work out," he continued. "That is, if you want it bad enough; but even wanting it takes time. Someday you'll turn the corner and see all the way down the street. It really works that way. You'll see, and don't brood so much."

She was aware that Mark had dismissed the subject, and her heart felt heavy. Her indescribable feelings had not yet been put into words and she had to turn some corner before she even knew what they were. No wonder Mark wanted to be a writer—he was so good at being obscure.

"Tell me about Stella," she said. "Are her parents mad too?"

Mark squashed his cigarette and his face became serious, almost sad. "Stella's parents were killed by the Nazis. She was only a baby and was smuggled out of Hungary to France, and when she was older she was sent to Israel and afterward, several years later, to a maiden aunt in Madison, Wisconsin. The aunt died when Stella was seventeen and from then on Stella worked, went to college nights, did everything on her own. I met her at the library at school."

"Oh, Mark, that's terrible. Didn't Mom and Dad feel sorry for her?"

Mark frowned. "No, I didn't tell them the whole story. I don't want them to feel sorry for her; I want them to accept her as a person, not as a charity case. She's my girl and I'd love her if she had thousands of thirty-second cousins."

"I'm sorry, Mark. I didn't mean it that way. I'm glad for you." She looked down at the floor then, in silence. She wondered how it would feel to be completely on her own, now at seventeen, like Stella. Would she make a terrible mess of her life, skid around on a sheet of ice, and stop moving altogether because she had taken a flop and was too scared to begin again? Stella must be unusual.

"She must be unusual," she said to Mark.

"She is," Mark answered with a special soft quality to his voice. He got up again, looked at his watch, and whistled. "It's almost one o'clock," he said, "and tonight's worn me out, too."

They said good night and Debby went to her room, where she kicked off her shoes and sat at the edge of her bed for a moment. Mark was free of all of them now, and the time would never come when they would fully understand each other. Mark did not seem to remember what it was like where she was, and she could not see down his street. She wondered what it felt like to pursue something as unwaveringly as Mark did his writing career, and Stella. It wasn't going to be easy for him, but he didn't seem to care! In fact, when he talked about both there was an excitement in his face, an eagerness that held no fear or uncertainty. He was so perfectly confident—as though his being a writer was already a fact, and his love for Stella a conclusion that needed no acceptance from others. What made the difference and why did she, in contrast, feel so weak, so afraid?

94

Then she recalled Mr. Stewart's appraisal of her playing, the shock of it and the anger, and finally the terrible
hollow incredulity that was too painful to think about.
She got up and went to the mirror, where she brushed
her hair hard until the electricity in it crackled. Her
image was flushed and far from sleepy-looking, and she
remembered suddenly how Josh had kissed her. What
was it that she felt for him; for anyone, in fact, and Steve
Randall in particular? She had only to close her eyes and
she could see Steve—tall, slim, and blue-eyed—smiling
down at her, watching her, staring at her, and herself
staring back tongue-tied, breathless almost. What was
it in her that made her comfortable and happy with Josh
but made her tense when she saw Steve Randall, pulled
at her like a loose wire getting taut and ready to spring?
She felt herself getting warm as she thought about it and
she turned quickly from the mirror to hang her clothes
in the closet. In back of her everyday clothes was a trans-
parent bag with a blue silk dress hanging in it. As soon
as her eye caught it, she knew she would wear it to the
dance tomorrow night and in seconds she had it out of
the bag and over her head, straining around in back to
pull up the zipper. The dress had a soft wide skirt falling
from a tight cummerbund, and the neckline was scooped
and gathered to a peasant-blouse effect. She had bought
it for Midge's confirmation party last year and had not
worn it since.

She went to the mirror again, lifted her arms, and began to sway in rhythm to the music sounding inside her,

95

watching from the corners of her eyes the way the skirt billowed and followed the motions of her body. How long it had been since she danced, and how desperately she had missed it! But tomorrow night she would dance again and maybe, just on the slimmest chance, there would be a Paul Jones and she would land Steve Randall for a partner. But no, if you thought about a thing like that beforehand it would never happen. Coincidences were not premeditated. Yet perhaps she could suggest a Paul Jones to Madie, who was in charge of the records. While she and Elly were putting the last touches to the decorations before the dance, she might say to Madie, casually, "Why don't we have a Paul Jones—good mixer, don't you think?

If only luck was with her, it might happen; but luck was something you couldn't count on, not if your name was Deborah Rose.

Eight

~~~~~~

The blue silk dress felt cool and soft against her skin, and at the slightest turn the billowing skirt swirled around her legs giving her a sense of weightlessness. It was wonderful to be dancing again, even if it was only Tom Harris who was her partner. Tom was her partner in biology lab too, the one who held the frogs for her and teased about them. Tom would hold the frog upside down by a leg, jiggle it, and laugh. "There it goes," he would say. "It's gonna get you; it's moving, ha, ha . . . moving, moving . . . ha, ha, ha." Tom was magnificent —a godsend who asked her to dance only minutes after she arrived at the dance, saving her the shame, the sheer torture, of standing there alone, all decked out with no place to go. Good old Tom Harris, dear Tom Harris, who deserved to be remembered in wills and honored in ser- mons. Who cared that he was gangly and awkward? He was someone to lead her around, and the litheness in herself would carry the rest. She had had the frothy feel- ing from the time she had taken a last look at herself in the mirror at home; seen the low, scooped neckline of the blue silk softly molded to her shoulders, and the highlights of her hair glistening like mahogany. She had asked herself then whether there would ever be another moment in life when she would feel truly beautiful.

"You're a good dancer," Tom Harris said.

"Thanks, Tom. So are you."

"Me? Ha, ha, ha. I'm better with frogs—like them better, anyway."

"You can't really compare the two," she said.

"Sure can't. I get a charge out of biology, but all I get out of dancing is sore muscles from keeping my back so stiff. I can't seem to loosen up, either. Excuse me . . . almost lost you there . . . guess I didn't do you much of a favor by asking you to dance."

If the darling only knew, she thought. "Why, you're an excellent dancer, Tom; really you are."

He grunted and they plodded on, independent of the music's tempo.

The gym was filling up now; but the room was large enough so that all the couples were distinguishable and anyone standing against the wall was clearly on display, like a marionette hanging limp from the roof of its little stage. Long Jean stood there in a straight-lined gray dress that made her look longer, and the expression on her face accented her starkness—adding to Debby's own misery at having to join her there, the two of them like Tweedle Dum and Tweedle Dee. Tom was definitely not going to keep this up. She tripped on his foot and he groaned; but he said laughingly that it was okay, that it made him feel better to know he wasn't the only clumsy galoot.

She searched furtively for Josh over Tom's shoulder. Where in the world was he? He said he would be here; he was supposed to take her home—Oh, of all times, why was he late tonight?

Tom danced her over in long, ungraceful strides to the refreshment table, which was decked out in gold crepe paper. A punch bowl stood in the center, and several heaping platters of sandwiches were covered with white paper napkins. Tom peaked under a napkin.

"Man," he said, "ham salad! Wish they'd get the dancing over with so we could eat."

She saw Josh then, and her gay mood returned; she could smile at Tom once more. At least, with Josh here she would not go home with deep hangnail hurts and the humiliation of the wall twisting in her insides like a creeper vine. Josh saw her too, and waved from across the room. He looked handsome in an olive-green corduroy jacket and gray slacks; wonderfully casual and self-assured, not cocky, merely comfortable. She wished he would cut in; but that was not fair to Tom Harris, who had rescued her from horrors. Josh kept his distance, watching her with a relaxed smile while he talked to Long Jean; leading her out to the floor, finally to finish the dance.

"Thanks, Debby," Tom Harris said when the dance finally ended. "Maybe we could have a sandwich together later on. Okay?"

99

"Okay," she answered, chuckling while Josh approached her. Long Jean had obviously disappeared when the dance ended.

Josh circled her waist lightly; she could hardly feel his touch as they danced together. "Decorations are terrific," he said. "Didn't you make some of them?"

"Yep. The sea nymphs." She laughed. "I copied them out of a tuna-fish ad. They're lopsided, I think."

Josh lopped his head to one side the better to observe the sea nymphs that were pinned to crinkled blue crepe paper and covered over with fishnet.

"They're good," he said. "Reminds me of tuna fish."

"Nasty boy. I'm a virtual Picasso."

"Poor girl; you'll die unsung."

"Better to die unsung than undanced with. What kept you so long?"

"Family problems. Dad wanted to talk."

"Nothing wrong where you're concerned, I hope?"

"Nothing serious. Dad doesn't get the time to sit me down very often, and tonight's his night off. He wants me to go to Northwestern for pre-med and med school. I had my heart set on an Eastern school—I've hardly ever been out of the Midwest—but it's all settled now."

"You're going East," she said, remembering their own family crisis with Mark. She assumed automatically that Josh had asserted himself.

"Nope. Going to Northwestern. Dad's friends are there."

"Why do you need your Dad's friends?" She was sorry

as soon as she said it. Josh's affairs with his family were no business of hers, but she felt strangely let down by his easy capitulation. It was true that Mark was older than Josh and had had four years of college to grow up in, but even when Mark was in high school he had never promised Dad anything; he had only said, "We'll see." And he had never taken the easy way out, even to accepting money from Dad to supplement his scholarship, but had preferred to work at odd jobs instead. In contrast to Mark, there was something spongy and soft in the way Josh reconciled what he wanted for himself with what he was told was best. But it was none of her business and, if Josh was satisfied, what right had she to question it?

"It's not that I *need* my Dad's friends," he said. "But Dad's right. Why make life tough when it can be easier? What will it prove?"

"Oh," she said, and then added on a sudden impulse, "Do you want terribly to be a doctor, Josh?"

He laughed. "Why so dramatic? I'm *planning* to be a doctor and, I hope, a good one; anyway, I've been around the stuff for so long I've always taken it for granted. When I entered high school, Dad told me to take all the chemistry and biology I could get because I'd be taking over his practice someday; I've never thought any more about it—Say . . . there's Steve!"

She looked up sharply as though someone had snapped off the light. Josh noticed her sudden movement and her face grew warm under his puzzled gaze.

"Holy smokes," he said. "Don't let her bother you *that* much."

For a moment she was confused, and then with a sense of relief she realized that Josh was referring to Pat Hamilton coming through the door on Steve's arm. She was wearing a green sheath dress that made her look taller and older; her hair was pulled back from her face, adding to the effect of maturity, and her expression was serene and self-assured. She and Steve looked so right together.

Debby stiffened in Josh's arms. The buoyancy she had felt earlier in the evening was gone, and in its place was an aching wish to go home. If she were grateful for anything though, it was that she had not had the courage to mention the Paul Jones to Madie earlier that afternoon. She had almost said it; but Elly had chattered interminably about where to put the sea nymphs, and whether they should go over the fishnet or under, and then suddenly Madie had finished organizing the records and was saying good-by. She was left with the words almost said, still tickling at her tongue. But she was glad now; the last thing she wanted was to dance with Steve, grow mute again when he came close to her, and give him something more to laugh about.

She glanced at him once more. His shoulders were slightly bent on his tall frame as he chatted with some of the people around him. He was lean and warm-looking.

The music spun its last bars, and her dance with Josh was ended. Elly rushed up while they were still in the middle of the floor. She smiled at both of them, but her attention focused on Josh.

"Aren't they gorgeous?" she said, exuding a drummed-up breathlessness.

"They certainly go well together," Debby answered, trying to sound nonchalant.

"I told you so. They go better under the fishnet."

"The fishnet! Oh, the decorations you mean."

"Of course, the decorations. What's the matter with you?"

Josh looked curious, but he said nothing. Elly latched onto his arm. "Don't think I'll let Debby monopolize you," she said. "This is our dance, remember?"

"That's right," Josh said, smiling. "Mind if I escort this lady back to the receiving line first?"

The receiving line, Debby thought. The wall, he meant. She cringed inwardly. Darn Elly, anyway. But that wasn't fair, either.

Josh and Elly left her standing alone near the sea nymphs. Even Long Jean was dancing with someone. When the music began she stood there for a moment wondering whether she should take refuge in the locker room or go over to the refreshment table, where Tom Harris stood like a sentinel over the sandwiches. She *had* promised to see him later, hadn't she? She moved toward him, keeping close to the wall so she wouldn't bump into the couples dancing. Pat Hamilton and Steve moved past her, and then a tall fellow she knew from her English class, but whose name she could never remember, cut in

103

on Pat. Steve disappeared in the other direction.

"Hi," she said, finally reaching Tom. "Still hungry?"

"Sure. Aren't you?" She wished he would show some enthusiasm about her joining him.

"Not hungry, yet," she answered. "Have you . . . uh . . . sworn off dancing, Tom?" What a stupid leading question, and what next?

"Yep," he said. "My back is stiffer than a—Hi, Steve!"

He had come up behind her and Tom had seen him first. When she turned, his hand was on her shoulder. "Dance?" he asked, and then looked at Tom. "Haven't booked her, have you, Tom?"

"Golly, no . . . my back can't hardly move at all."

Steve laughed, and then she was in his arms. She felt him tighten his clasp around her waist; his cheek brushed her forehead, and for a long while they moved together silently, very close, as though there were no one else in the room. She was afraid he would hear her heartbeat and she pulled slightly away; but he was unyielding, and she felt she had to find something to say or he would discover the warmth that was spreading and enveloping her like an umbrella being opened.

"It's a nice dance, isn't it?" Her voice was unnatural, half its usual volume.

"Now it is," he answered softly. The umbrella snapped open.

"B-better than bumping into each other all the time, don't you think?"

"Much better, now that I'm holding you." Silence

again. But this time she did not care if he discovered her heartbeat or not. The blue silk dress was air around her; she had no feet or arms, and the sea nymphs danced on the walls.

"I have something for you," he said, loosening his hold. "I think you'll like it; anyway, I hope so."

She looked up at him.

"Will you meet me later . . . around eleven-thirty in front of your house? I have to take Pat home, but I want to give you this thing. I'll have my car."

It was happening too fast. After weeks of nothing, suddenly it was as though a bonfire was blazing out of control.

"I—don't think I can. Josh asked to take me home. I said I would . . ."

There was an urgency in his voice that penetrated and made her feel urgent too. "He can still take you home."

"I don't know. I want to . . . but, Josh—"

"You can send him away early and wait for me, eleven-thirty in front of your house. Debby, please . . ."

Her thoughts reeled as his arm tightened around her again. She would have to tell Josh she couldn't go for hamburgers and shakes after the dance, and it would be awkward not asking him into the house. What was it Steve had for her and, oh, what miracle made him notice her! But sending Josh away, lying to him, went against the grain, somehow.

The last refrains of music were spinning on the disk and she and Steve would not be together much longer;

105

she wanted to be with him so terribly. His cheek brushed her hair again and the pressure of his hand was warm in hers. She whispered to him, "Yes . . . I'll wait for you."

The locker room was empty when she went in to repair her lipstick and comb her hair before leaving the dance with Josh. Sandwiches and punch were being served in the gym and Tom Harris was enjoying himself at last. She chuckled, remembering the sober and deliberate way he had attacked the business of eating: first one sandwich, then another, and another. Frogman Harris, she sang to herself, I love you. She loved everyone—even Elly, with whom she had had to share Josh; and Bill Washburn, who had danced without uttering a word to her throughout; and Chip Hendricks, who danced fast no matter what the tempo of the music. And there *had* been a Paul Jones after all, but she had not landed Steve for it. Funny, funny, funny how nothing was neat or normal tonight.

She slipped the comb through her hair, smiling at her own flushed image in the mirror. What could Steve have for her? After that first dance he had not asked her again; but they had brushed past each other in the arms of other partners, and they had exchanged looks with fresh meaning now—looks that said the evening still held something wonderful in store for them. Pat Hamilton, willowy as a spring flower, leaned against him possessively, but to Debby she had dwindled in stature. She was no longer the Venus of the gym, but only a girl at a school dance.

The door swung open and Elly came in to stand beside her at the mirror.

"Wait for me," she said, taking her comb and lipstick out.

Debby watched while Elly ran the comb through her dark hair. "The dance was a success, don't you think, and you were right about the decorations."

"Mmmmm-hmmmm," Elly answered, smoothing her lipstick on. The two girls looked at each other's reflection in the mirror. Elly was strangely silent, as though something was on her mind. It wasn't like her.

"Steve Randall asked you to dance," she said, turning away from the mirror at last. "Well, I guess it's none of my business—"

"Only half a dance," Debby said. "Is there something wrong with that?"

Elly answered as though she had an unpleasant duty to dispense, "Pat Hamilton really has it in for you."

Debby felt her face get hot and tried to sound indifferent so Elly would not suspect anything. "Why? It was only a dance. He danced with plenty of other girls besides Pat."

"Not the way he danced with you," Elly said, accenting the word "you."

"I didn't realize I was being watched so closely."

"This is a small school, Debby, and North Haven isn't the same as the South Side."

"What do you mean by that? What does the South Side have to do with it?"

107

"Don't get mad, for heaven's sake. I'm just trying to be a friend. I overheard Angie and Pat, that's all. Steve was in earshot too. He must have overheard. Angie was saying that Steve wanted to try out a new product from the South Side, where they're free and easy. You should have heard Pat laugh. I'm almost *sure* Steve overheard. I didn't want to look at him; after all, I wasn't supposed to be hearing this conversation."

"That's garbage—rotten garbage—and maybe you *were* supposed to hear. Maybe it was said just for you, so you'd be sure to behave with the upper classes."

"Just a minute now, my friend. I've never had any trouble with those girls before you showed up. They go their way and I go mine. A person would have to be pretty thick not to see what was going on out on that dance floor. I'm afraid I agree with them . . . and frankly, Debby, I think Steve *is* interested in the kind of stuff that's supposed to go on in the South Side. I just don't want to see you make a sap of yourself."

The door of the locker room swung open again and several girls came in.

"Coming, Debby?" Elly asked her.

"Go ahead," she answered. "I—I have to straighten my hose."

She walked toward the back of the locker room and sank down on a small bench inside a booth. She could think of one thing only—that everyone had noticed them dancing together, and that Steve had done it deliberately. A sudden memory of his closeness came over her and she drew her breath in sharply, remembering how she had succumbed. Maybe they were right; maybe he had wanted to test a South Side product. Where had she left her good sense? She had given Pat and her side-kick, Angie, ammunition to barrage her and the South Side with labels, laugh at her, ridicule her. And Elly, poor Elly, was afraid it might affect her too. But Steve had not made it appear that way; his voice was sweet and urgent and she had believed him completely. Oh, God, she thought, and then the silent choked-off sobs began to come. Why, she asked herself, does everything I touch turn out this way?

It was almost ten minutes before the locker room was clear and she could come out of the booth without meeting anyone. She washed her face, applied her powder carefully, and went out to Josh, who was leaning against the door of the half-empty gym, still waiting.

"Holy smokes!" he said. "Do you always take so much time combing your hair?"

"I felt a little sick," she said. "The ham salad, maybe."

"Want to go right home?"

"I think I'd better . . . I'm sorry, Josh. I hope I didn't ruin your evening."

Nine

The following morning Debby got out of bed feeling tired and drained. She had spent the better part of the night reliving the moments she had spent with Steve, and the conversation with Elly. She had lain there with her eyes closed, her thoughts bouncing from the one incident to the other, then mixing the two together and trying, afterward, to separate them, until her head began to pound and she had gotten up to get a drink of water.

Her headache was somewhat better now, but the thought of chatting with the family made her want to get back into bed and stay there. She slipped a skirt and blouse on hurriedly and went into the bathroom, where she spread a wet cold washcloth over her face and held it there for a few minutes before going downstairs.

Mark, Dad, and Grandpa were seated around the kitchen table and Mother was rushing around the kitchen preparing turkey sandwiches for Mark's trip back to Wisconsin and watching the pancakes on the grill at the same time. Mark's long legs jutted out from under the

110

table and he leaned back in his chair, tipping it slightly while he drank his coffee. It was apparent from his peaceful, happy air that he had finally brought Dad around, or at least gotten him to realize that he wasn't going to be talked out of Stella or a career in writing. Dad sat there watching Mark eat, an air of quiet acquiescence about him while he drank his coffee.

When Mark saw her come in he tipped his coffee cup to her. "Heard you come in last night," he said. "Did you knock 'em dead?"

"Oh, sure," she muttered, bringing a plate of pancakes to the table. "There are corpses all over the gym." Even to herself her voice sounded strained and a bit tremulous.

"That's what I figured."

She was aware of the silence that followed, of Mother turning to look at her from the counter near the window, of Dad's curious glance, and of Grandpa rolling a cigarette between his thumb and forefinger.

"It was okay," she said. "Well . . . you remember what school dances are like . . . kind of sappy, that's all."

Mark's eyebrows went up, and then his expression changed to one of detachment. "Do I remember?" he singsonged. "Man, oh, man, I sure do. The best thing about graduating from high school was the parole from school dances. I'd 've r-r-rither died thin go to an-ither-r-r."

"What's so terrible about them?" Grandpa asked.

Marked winked at her before answering. "You just

111

wouldn't understand, Grandpa. You just wouldn't understand."

Dear Mark, she thought to herself. He had guessed, and he was letting her off the hook. Mother and Dad laughed at him, and the subject of the school dance was dropped.

"Say," Mark said, looking at his watch, "it's almost eleven o'clock. I promised Stella I'd be back to take her to dinner. She's pretty anxious to hear how things worked out." He glanced sidelong at Dad while he got up from the chair. "Can't wait to tell her what good sports you've been."

With the excuse of homework she could spend the rest of the day in her room without further explanation. She was profoundly grateful for that, but when she sat down at her desk, her algebra book and a pad of paper before her, she could not concentrate on them; her eyes kept lifting to the window, where the yard lay stretched beyond the pane. It was almost the middle of November, but today was warm and copper-bright. Only a few days ago it snowed a bit, but within hours all the symptoms of winter disappeared and Indian summer exhaled its last fragile breath. The yard was covered with moist and tarnished leaves, but patches of gray-green grass poked through as though reaching for the unexpected burst of sunlight. It was a day to covet, a mild and glowing day that might not come again until spring.

She sat there, staring through the window, trancelike.

There was a bleakness inside her, and a dull monotonous ache—the residue of last night's humiliation. She began to doodle on the pad of paper in front of her . . . and when she found herself drawing circles within circles within circles, she tore the sheet from the pad and tossed it into the wastebasket. She glanced at her algebra book, flipped a few pages absently, and then closed it. She could not think about algebra today.

She heard Mother call her in a shrill voice as though she had been trying to rouse her for a long time. "*Debby* . . . will you *please* come to the phone?"

The first thing that entered her mind was that it might be Steve; but she dismissed the idea, grunting at herself in disgust. What was the matter with her? Hadn't she had enough? Yet, in spite of it, she came down the steps trembling inside.

"Hello," she said quietly into the mouthpiece.

"Debby?" The voice from the other end of the line was from another world. "It's Jessie. Jessie Perkins."

"Jessie! It's so good to hear from you. I've been meaning to call you, but things have been so . . . so . . . How are you . . . and Midge, how's Midge? I haven't talked to her for ages. . . . Oh, it's so good to hear from you!" She stopped, breathless.

Jessie laughed with high-pitched excitement. "We're all fine . . . everybody misses you like the very blue blazes. Debby . . . I have something to tell you . . . something wonderful." It was Jessie who sounded breathless now.

"You're singing solo graduation night!"

"Not exactly. I might do that too . . . but this is better, much better."

"What is it, Jess? Tell me before I bust!"

"The Purcell scholarship! The auditions are in February and I'm going to get a chance at it. Mr. Mason told me to start working right now."

For a moment she could not speak. The words "Purcell scholarship" stood out from the rest as though they had a dimension of their own, unrelated to anyone but herself. She had come to think of the scholarship as something out of all human reach, like the doll she had seen in a store when she was a child—the doll that had blond hair and blue eyes with eyelashes, and a pale pink organdy dress with a red velvet sash. She had longed to take it from its shelf, feel the organdy dress and the smooth, warm texture of the velvet; but Mother had said no, they could not afford the doll, that she had better find something within her reach. She had left the store, her hand tightly held by Mother's, looking back at the beautiful doll on the shelf while every step carried her farther and farther from what was hers by every right; and yet, not hers. She had never considered the possibility that the doll might be bought by someone else.

The voice on the other end of the line called to her anxiously. "Debby, are you still there?"

"Oh. Yes . . . of course I'm here. Congratulations, Jess. I . . . you'll win it; I know you will."

"But I get so nervous," Jessie said. "Remember that time at church I thought I would faint before my solo?"

"You sang beautifully . . . you know you did."

"My voice broke at the end." Jessie sounded close to tears. "If it breaks this time, I won't win . . . you know what the Purcell standards are. I'm so worried about the audition I can hardly sleep nights . . . and it's only November."

"Your voice won't break. You'll see." A wave of compassion for her friend overcame her momentarily. Jessie never had much self-confidence. Maybe that was the reason she spent more time at the Settlement House than she did in practicing voice; maybe Jessie, like herself, was afraid to get too deeply involved, only to get hurt. Poor Jessie. It was harder for her. Negroes on the South Side of Chicago had two labels—either they were intellectuals and more was expected of them than white intellectuals, or they were branded tough, delinquent, and dangerous. No wonder Jessie was timid, lacking in confidence.

"I wish I could help," she said impulsively.

"Would you . . . oh, Debby, would you?"

"B-but how? I don't see how I—"

"I talked to Mr. Mason and he said it would be fine . . . in fact, he was very happy about it. He said it might help you too."

"Will you please tell me what you're talking about?"

"About your being my accompanist. I won't be so nervous if you're there . . . when you accompanied me before, I always did my best. Please, Debby, I'll be so grateful to you."

Her mind stuck on Mr. Mason's saying it might help

her to accompany Jessie. What could he mean? How could her presence at the Purcell auditions be anything but agonizing? She couldn't do it. Not for Jessie, not for anyone. She wanted to hang up the phone and brush away the web that was beginning to spin around her. "I can't, Jessie. I'm out of practice. I haven't touched the piano . . ."

Jessie was suddenly apologetic. "Debby, I'm sorry. I know what the scholarship meant to you, but I thought since you weren't eligible anyway . . . Oh, I feel awful . . . I guess I wanted to win so badly I never stopped to think. Are you angry, Deb?"

"No, of course not. It's not anything like that," she lied. "I'm afraid I'll hold you back, that's all."

"If that's all it is, you know you won't hold me back. I won't feel so scared and alone if you're there with me."

The words slipped out before she could stop them. "Okay," she said. "Let's try . . . I only hope it works."

Jessie used superlatives in thanking her and they spent the rest of the conversation in making arrangements.

She hung up the phone and stood there for a moment, wiping her moist, clammy hands against the side of her dress. Then, in an abrupt sudden turn, she ran up the steps to her room and pulled a white sweater off the hanger in her closet. The only thing she could think of was getting away, out of the house, somewhere she could be alone.

Downstairs she found Mother and told her she was going for a walk, and then quickly, before she could ask about the phone call, was outdoors in the sun-bright day. She slipped her arms through the sweater and glanced around, wondering in which direction to walk, and then, deciding on the beach, she headed east.

She had not gone more than a few steps when she looked up to the blaring sound of a car horn. A small foreign sports model pulled up to the curb and Steve Randall leaned over the front seat calling to her through the open window. "I've been driving around your block for half an hour," he said. "I was hoping you'd be out."

She stopped, wondering whether she should walk off without speaking to him or make some excuse. He opened the door of the car and sat waiting with a puzzled expression on his face while he watched her hesitate on the sidewalk. She forced herself to smile. Why should she show him she cared enough to be angry?

"I can't," she said, meticulously casual. "I have another appointment and I'm late."

"I waited for almost an hour last night."

"I'm sorry." She could not look at him and concentrated, instead, on the sleek little sports car, its soft cream color glistening in the sun. Had he planned to impress her with it, bowl her over? After all, a crude South Side girl was not supposed to be accustomed to such fine things.

"I'm really late," she repeated. "I have to go."

He stared at her and for a moment when their eyes met she thought he looked hurt, but she turned away quickly and walked off.

117

On the beach she slipped off her shoes and socks and buttoned her sweater against the fresh wind blowing off the lake that made the sand under her feet cold and moist. She climbed up to the concrete pier and walked out to the very end, where she sat down and swung her legs over the edge. She sat there motionless, watching the milky surf tumble over, recede, and build up again with a hissing rush that finally exhausted itself in a limp slap against the sand. Three sailboats bobbed gull-like on the horizon and she wondered idly what it was like in a sailboat on a windy day, plowing the active water with the spray against one's face and vistas of beautiful freedom all around like music with the sound of the surf and the gulls' shrill clucking and the rhythm of the water against the sky. What would it be? Something uncluttered and sure of itself, powerful, yet full of melody, like Greek statues and paintings by Gaugin. Not Chopin; he would spoil it with too many trills.

Someone tapped her shoulder. She turned sharply and looked up to Steve Randall, standing barefoot on the pier beside her.

"It's a free country," he said, and sat down. "Did your appointment think you weren't coming? That kind of puts him in a class with me, doesn't it?"

She looked him full in the face. "I'm not like that," she said.

"You're not? Now whatever gave me the impression . . ."

She pulled her legs up over the pier and started to

rise, but Steve's arm on hers held her back. What was he trying to do? Why didn't he give up on her? Hadn't she made it clear that South Side products were not as free and easy as he imagined? She looked at his face. It was a strong, clean-looking face, and his blue eyes had no suggestion of sarcasm or malice. She averted her eyes before he became conscious of her staring; the drum inside her was beginning to respond.

"Why didn't you wait last night?" He asked her softly.

What could she tell him without sounding like a fool? "I—I didn't feel well. Josh took me home."

"Did Pat say something to you, something sweet, like that time in the drugstore?"

She pulled her arm away. "Pat Hamilton considers it beneath her to speak to me; so does Angie. You have lovely friends."

Steve smiled. "Don't you think," he said, as though he had not heard her remark, "that 'Angie Kress' sounds like a brand of cheese? What kind would you say she was, cheddar . . . pimento . . . swiss maybe, with holes in it to see through?" He moved closer to her and put his hand on her arm again. "Want to see what I brought for you?"

The water splashed against the pier, and the spray doused both of them. Steve pulled her to her feet and walked her to his car parked in the circle overlooking the beach. He dumped their shoes into the back seat and took a flat package off the shelf. She looked curiously at it while he took her arm and led her into the park, where

119

they sat down on the leaf-strewn brown-gold grass. His fingers seemed tremulous as he unwrapped the package, and she watched him while the drum inside her beat steadily against her ribs.

When the wrapping was off, she gasped. "Steve! Did you do that?"

He had uncovered a small canvas stretched and tacked to a frame about twelve inches square. On it was painted the face of a girl—a girl whom she recognized as herself in the crew-necked jersey she wore when she played tennis. The head and shoulders were erect, but the face was pale and small for the large wistful eyes and the full unsmiling mouth. The deep red hair blazed in all directions from the face, giving the otherwise real-istic features a free and impressionistic air.

"It's beautiful—oh, it's lovely! You did paint it, didn't you? You're an artist. Imagine that! An artist!"

She held the canvas up and studied it. The girl he had painted was not conventionally beautiful, but she was sensitive and, at the same time, striking. Did he really see her like that? Oh, it was too perfect to think that he was an artist—and she a musician. No wonder they were drawn toward each other, like osmosis, or magic, or something entirely beyond belief but nevertheless true.

She sighed, holding the canvas at arm's length. "Am I really like that?"

He took the picture from her and put it down on the grass beside them while he moved closer and covered her hands with his. "To me, you are," he said. "You're th

120

first person or thing I've wanted to paint since they made me stop."

"*Who* made you stop?"

"Maybe I shouldn't say they made me stop, but they made me feel foolish about it. They even wanted me to see a psychologist when I quit drawing horses and boats and started abstracts in oils. They said I had better come down to earth, stop thinking wild thoughts—"

"Who? Who? I can't imagine anyone discouraging you like that."

"My parents."

"Your parents! Why, I think they should be proud. How could they be anything but proud?"

"My old man would be prouder if I had stayed a basketball hero. I'm not trying to give the impression that they're not nice people; they're just conventional. They want me to fit in."

"Fit in to what?"

"Oh, law school, Yale . . . let's not talk about it." His hand clasped hers tightly now. "It's enough that I saw you in the drugstore and wanted to paint again." He ran his fingers through her hair. "I've never seen hair that color," he whispered. "Like an Irish Setter . . ." They laughed, and his face was so close to hers she could feel his breath on her cheek, and then she was in his arms and he was kissing her and holding her hard against him. The heartache of her conversation with Jessie dissolved; all the pain of the past months evaporated; the only thing that meant anything now was Steve's whispering against

121

her temple, "Debby, Debby, I thought I'd fallen in love with a portrait; but when we danced last night . . ."

He held her close and kissed her again and again.

When she got home, Dad was in the hall. "It's raining," he said. "Where've you been without a coat?"

"Just walking." She saw him glance at the package under her arm.

"Alone?" he asked.

"Uh . . . yes, alone."

Later, when she thought about it, she had an uneasy feeling; she could not figure out why she had lied.

Ten

The weeks following were out of a storybook. She had never conceived of such happiness, nor thought the kind of feelings she had for Steve were possible. She had had crushes before; she had even imagined herself in love with Tony Mescuto once, and then with Josh; but now, by comparison, she knew that what she had felt for each of them was childish, meaningless. When Steve held her in his arms she wanted to stop breathing; she wanted the world to stop moving and hold the two of them suspended forever.

Every day after school they would go for a drive in Steve's car, ending up usually in the park near the lake. It was December now, but the weather was still mild enough so they could walk and even sit on the grass.

It was a particularly sunny day when they walked out to the end of the pier again.

"It's almost like an anniversary," Steve said, pulling her close to him.

"I know. Four weeks now."

"Have you ever been in love for four whole weeks before?" he asked.

She laughed. "Nope. Don't think so. How about you?"

He shook his head.

"What about Pat?" she asked.

"Jealous?"

"No, but I sort of worry about her sometimes. The looks she gives me in class make me feel I'm doing something awful to her."

"I'll bet she's mad all right, but don't think she's hurt because she's in love with me; it's a clear-cut case of real estate, property rights, that's all."

"I can't imagine anyone thinking about a person like that. She *must* love you or she wouldn't feel that you're her—her property."

"Well, maybe she does in her way . . . but it has to be *her* way. Remember how mad she was when I was politely retired from the basketball team? That's typical of Pat. Whatever I do has to make her feel big; and when I don't measure up, she's mad. One time I told her I would rather go to art school than to Yale. She practically flipped because she's planning to go to a girl's school close to New Haven. See what I mean?"

"If she'd ever seen any of your paintings, I'll bet she'd feel differently."

"Oh, she's seen them. I can't say they knocked her dead—she thought some of them were cute."

"Cute! You're kidding me now, aren't you?"

"No. I'm not kidding. Everything to Pat is either cute or disgusting. It has to be one or the other. Say, what are we talking about Pat for—wasting all this time before the sun goes down?" He drew her closer and whispered against her lips, "I love you, Debby. I love you, I love you." She felt his lips warm and hard on hers and she tightened her arms around his neck, responding with all her heart.

Afterward, on the way home, she asked him to come into the house. He had come in only once, when he took her to a movie, and then he had only stood in the hallway close to the door while she introduced him to Mother and Dad.

"I wish you'd come in for a minute. Mom is beginning to wonder where I go every day after school."

"Did you tell her?" he asked with a peculiar, quick urgency.

"Well . . . no . . . I don't know why not, but I didn't."

"It's better that way," Steve said. "For a while, any-way."

"But why?"

"Things get complicated when mothers get involved. Why don't we just keep it between us for a while—until, well, until I straighten things out. My mother is crazy about Pat; we have the same background and all, and my folks aren't keen on my mixing with—"

"With what?" She interrupted him hotly.

"Forget it, Debby. Can't we keep things the way they are for a while, seeing each other after school? Can't you tell your mother that you have to work in the library?"

"I've never done that before, Steve—I mean lying like that."

"You won't have to for long—just for a while, to avoid things happening like that night I took you to the movies."

"What happened? I wasn't aware of anything happening."

"Maybe you weren't, but a friend of my mother's was sitting right in back of us . . . This is a small town, Debby."

"You mean you were ashamed or something?" She felt a funny pang like the one just before you got sick to your stomach, but Steve took her hand and held it while he steered the car with the other.

"No," he said sharply. "Don't think stuff like that. It's only that I have to work things out before the crows descend on my folks. Listen, I'll tell you what. New Year's is two weeks off. Let's make that the beginning. Okay? I'll have a talk with my folks and then we can go everywhere together." He rounded the corner to her street and pulled up in front of her house. "Debby," he said, turning off the motor. "I want you to go steady with me. Will you?"

"Oh, Steve, do you really believe it will work out?"

"I know it will if you give me a little time. Two weeks? Okay?"

She smiled at him and then he kissed her lightly on the mouth. When she went into the house she felt lighthearted again. Mother was in the hallway and she sailed up and planted a kiss on her cheek, almost knocking her over.

"Goodness me!" Mother exclaimed, standing back. "To what do I owe—"

Debbie laughed. "Nothing. Just that dinner smells yummy. Fried chicken, hmmm?"

Mother stared at her. "No," she said. "Fish."

"I could have sworn it was fried chicken." Mother shook her head and handed her a large manila envelope from Jessie Perkins. "Are you and Jessie conducting some business?" she asked.

"I'll tell you about it later," Debby answered, and slid past Mother into the living room. "How's the book, Grandpa?"

He looked up and grunted. "A book is a book," he said. "It teaches you about life, so it can't be bad; but if it's a substitute for life, it can't be good."

"You can't win, can you, Grandpa?"

He sat quietly studying her face. "Your hair is beginning to grow long again," he said.

She put her hand up to her hair and mumbled, "Yes."

"I told you so," he said.

"You told me what?"

"That you couldn't keep it from growing."

"Grandpa, if I know you, we're going to go all the way to China before you say what you mean."

"Why should we go to China? You seem very happy in North Haven."

127

She flushed and averted her eyes. "You can't stay miserable forever. Anything wrong in that?"

"No, no," he answered. "That's good. And he's a handsome boy. There is something sensitive about his face."

"Grandpa! What are you talking about?"

He continued as though she knew quite well what he meant. "But why does he never come into the house? Poor boy. I can't forget how he stood in the hallway that one time, mumbling to your mother and father as though he were afraid to cross over the line. Yes, that is the trouble. He is afraid of us. He looked at me like I was brought here from a wax museum."

She got up with a start. "Grandpa. You have no right— Since when did you start interfering in my . . ." She stopped, and began again in what she was satisfied was a calmer tone of voice. "How this family blows things up! Dad had me practically married to Josh Sandow. If Mark wasn't going to be a doctor, I had to be the doctor's wife. And now you. You don't know anything about Steve, and already you're making a big philosophical issue of it."

Grandpa shrugged and took out his cigarette case.

"All right. All right," he said. "I apologize to you, Deborah. But I would not like you to become afraid, like that boy."

She turned and started to leave the room. Halfway, she stopped and looked over her shoulder at Grandpa, who was still watching her while he puffed at his cigarette holder. "You don't *always* know the real story, Grandpa," she said. "Just remember that."

She took Jessie's envelope from where she had put it down on the hall table, went up the steps to her room and plunked down on her bed. Grandpa was impossible. How did he know so much anyway? Steve had been to the house only once and then he had hardly come past the door, but that was enough for Grandpa; a fleeting glimpse of Steve qualified him as an expert on human affairs. It was really best not to listen, not to think about it. She sat up and tore open the envelope.

The music Jessie had chosen was the spiritual "Every Time I Feel the Spirit" and a solo from a Bach oratorio. The spiritual would be no trouble, but the Bach! It was a whopper, blast it. Why had she told Jessie she would play? Why hadn't she had the guts to say no? The Bach solo required skill, musicianship, and she had not practiced, not laid a finger to the keys in months except for the fiasco with Mr. Stewart. Why did everyone harp on Bach? Who had chosen it for Jessie, anyway? Mr. Mason? She couldn't believe it. He was too democratic. He wasn't the kind of man who would stand over Jessie and fatuously pronounce, "Bach, Miss Perkins. Bach."

She hummed the first bars of the score and ended with a grunt. She would have to work it out. You could always count on Bach to make you sweat. Of all the gorgeous stuff to sing, Jessie had to pick this! She felt suddenly panicked. What if she messed it up? What if she threw Jessie off while she was singing, made her hesitate? The audition was to be tape-recorded and, once you got started, you had to grind ahead, mistakes included. She

129

would have to get some help, but from whom? Asking Mr. Mason for help would mean taking the train into Chicago after school, and then she would not have time for Steve. Stewart? she asked herself. My, how he would gloat, especially at her crawling to him with nothing less than a Bach score between her teeth. Well, let him. It was for Jessie, not for herself. If it were for herself, she could never give him the satisfaction; but she could do it for Jessie.

She slipped the Bach score under her arm; went down to the living room and opened the piano lid, placing the score on the rack. She sat down on the bench and put her fingers to the keys. Then she began, clumsily but clearly enough to get an idea of the stoic first chords. She felt the vibrations go through her stomach; but she continued, trying to sight-read the notes and count the beat at the same time. She knew it was not good, that it would take weeks to smooth it out; but she went on, caught up in the strangely compelling music.

Mother's voice behind jolted her to a stop. "Debby!" she shrieked. "You're playing! Can I believe my ears? You're playing!"

She swung around on the bench, catching a glimpse of Grandpa sitting on the sofa with the book open in his lap. A suggestion of a smile played around his eyes and mouth. Why, she hadn't even thought about his still being here when she came down to play.

"My word," she said to both of them, "why the hysterics? Haven't you ever heard me play before?"

130

He was sitting at his tidy desk when she came into the room and she noticed that he had on the same gray suit, the jacket all buttoned up again and his necktie impeccably straight.

"Good afternoon, Miss Rose," he said.

"Mr. Stewart . . ." she began. "I . . . well, I have some music here . . . a friend of mine is going to sing, and I'm planning to accompany her. I'd appreciate some help."

"I'd be very glad to help," he said, "if you're really serious about it."

She winced. There he went. No sooner did a cordial word come out of his mouth than he had to sprinkle it with cyanide.

"I wouldn't be here if I weren't serious," she snapped back—and then stopped herself from being rude, although the old crank deserved it. "I mean . . . I want to do the best I can."

He surprised her by smiling. "I imagine you do," he said, and nodded toward the music in her hands; his smile was suddenly gone, like a comedian pretending to have wiped it from his face. "What do you have there?"

She held out the score and he adjusted his horn-rimmed glasses. "Hmmmmm," he said, studying it. "You have a friend who plans to sing this?" He had emphasized the word "you" as though any friend of hers could not possibly accomplish such a thing.

She held herself back and managed to answer coolly,

131

"She is a very good singer. She is so good she is auditioning for the Purcell scholarship."

Mr. Stewart held up his hand. "All right," he said, "no need to get defensive. I didn't say she couldn't sing." Then his tone softened. "The Purcell scholarship, eh? Isn't that going to be a bit difficult for you?"

"Yes," she said, looking directly back at him. He wasn't going to beat her down again. If it killed her she would stand up to him. But he said no more; he got up from his desk and motioned her to the piano, while he placed the music on the rack.

She sat down on the bench and placed her fingers to the keys ready to play, but he stopped her brusquely by brushing her hands off again.

"Don't plunge as if you were going to dive into a tank. Look at the music, organize yourself. Think first, then play."

She should have known better than to come back to him, but she was here. Okay, she thought to herself. She'd get through it for Jessie's sake.

She looked at the music and tried to hear the tones and beat in her head before putting her fingers on the keys. It was a method she had never consciously employed before. Then she began to play. She was not entirely satisfied but, this time, she played through to the end. At least she had been able fully to concentrate on the music. Nothing else had been in her mind—not Steve, nor Mr. Stewart, nor even Jessie's voice, which would be singing above her accompaniment. No thoughts of twilight or green fields or lovers had stood between herself and the music; the music alone had carried her.

"Not too bad," Mr. Stewart said. "Not good; but at least you're getting somewhere, and it's obvious that you've practiced."

She took a deep breath and folded her hands in her lap. She hardly heard his remark because she knew now she could do it. Whatever Mr. Stewart said, she could do it.

"Are you willing to work?" he asked.

She nodded.

"Well, then," he said, "I'd still like you to do some Bach exercises before you try that number again. Your technique is clumsy. Your friend won't sing well if you slip those notes." He went to the file case and took a book of music from it. "Two hours a day," he said, holding it out to her, and then he added, "at least."

Her preoccupation had passed and she realized now what he was saying. Practice Bach exercises two hours a day! Was he joking?

"Mr. Stewart . . . I only came to get help with this."

"And I asked if you were serious."

"I am about playing for Jessie, but—"

"If you are, you'll work. Nothing comes easy. Not even when you're in the limelight."

"I'm not interested in being in the limelight."

"Miss Rose," he said finally, "if you're not willing to work *my* way, don't waste my time or yours. I'm willing to give you formal lessons, but I won't have you jumping

133

in and out of here whenever you feel like it."

She looked at him, trying to comprehend his meaning. Formal lessons for what? Just so she could accompany Jessie? Why was he willing to bother with her at all if he thought she was such a rotten, sloppy musician? Why was he willing to spend his time with her? Most likely because he made a hobby out of beating people down, lording it over them, and she was a ripe new candidate. She remembered how he had brushed her hands off the keys, and his biting sarcasm—"Don't plunge as if you were going to dive into a tank. Think first" . . . oh, boy, not on his life.

She took the book of exercises from him, thinking that it was best to take them and get out of here. She could return them some other time or, better yet, slip them into his box at the office.

"I'll try to work on them," she said.

"Good," he answered. "We'll have a lesson the first Tuesday after Christmas vacation. After school. Does that fit your schedule?"

"Oh, yes, that would be fine . . . and thank you so much." She muttered good-by and was out of the room.

For the entire hour before school let out, her second encounter with Mr. Stewart would not leave her mind. His offer to give her private lessons affected her as though she had swallowed a fly, and she wondered if he liked her playing more than she imagined. Anyway, she had never been so absorbed in a piece of music before, nor concentrated the way she had this afternoon. Never

134

had she felt such strength in her fingers or known a sense of exhilaration from the music itself. Mr. Stewart's approval or disapproval had not seemed to matter; the music was all she cared about. She wished school would be over quickly; she wanted to go home and get back to the piano, try it again, recapture the experience.

Then she remembered she had to meet Steve.

Eleven

Debby dumped her books in the back seat of Steve's car, pulled off her gloves, and held her hands up close to the heater.

"Whew," she said, "it's getting nippy."

"Might even snow for Christmas," he answered. "But I wouldn't count on it." His voice sounded peculiarly flat.

She looked at him while he released the brake and accelerated the motor. There was a tense, set look about him today. He pushed the gearshift up with impatient, tugging movements and the car spurted forward, throwing her back a little; something was wrong, but she suppressed the impulse to ask him.

When they got to the street where he ordinarily turned off to the beach road, he glanced over at it for a moment and then drove by without a word. He drove in silence, hardly shifting his eyes from the road, while she concentrated on the large houses of North Haven with their broad lawns, now soggy and bleak-looking; then they were at the edge of town where the houses were smaller, less cared for, and finally she felt the car bump over the tracks and out into the country.

Neither of them had spoken the whole time, but she could not bear it any longer. Maybe he was the kind of person who didn't need to talk; but she had to know why he had brought her here, why he seemed so awfully upset despite his silence.

"It might snow for Christmas after all," she said, hoping it would break the ice.

"Think so?" he answered, without turning his head.

"Steve . . . what's wrong . . . why?"

The car wheels screeched around a bend, and gravel beat against the fenders as the car straightened out and came to a stop on a side road where there were no houses. Empty fields were on either side of them, lifeless fields that she could not imagine plump with corn in summer. He leaned one arm over the steering wheel and looked at her. The whirring hum of the heater had been cut off, and the silence between them was heavy and unaccompanied.

She felt she would scream if he didn't say something, if he didn't act like himself again. Their afternoons together had been like a love song, achingly sweet and happy; but his present mood was surly, jarringly unfamiliar, a quality she couldn't name. She studied his face, trying to discover the answer, and then she heard him say her name in a voice neither whispered nor spoken.

She felt herself being pulled toward him, being held

tighter than he had ever held her before. There was a humming in her ears and she felt that in another moment her heart would stop; he kissed her, holding her hard against him, his face almost hurting hers.

Pulling away, she whispered "Steve! What's wrong?" and was startled once more by his short, rasping laugh.

"As a cave man," he murmured, looking away, "I'm a flop."

"What's wrong?" She repeated. "Tell me."

He rubbed the side of his jaw like someone who had just been hit.

"Everything's wrong."

"Is it school? Aren't you going to make it?"

"I'll make it. It isn't that." He hesitated for a moment, and then continued. "If you want to know, it's you—us."

She had expected it somehow and had braced herself, hoping—yet, when it came, the blow was as though she had been taken completely off guard.

"My father is sore as blazes," he said. "Pat spilled the story to her mother, about my going with a Jewish girl— a South Side beatnik was her version. So my mother had tea with Mrs. Hamilton and, let me tell you, it's a mess. Pat's not the kind of girl to let something die; anyway, our families have been buddies from way back—probably before the *Mayflower* even got here. I can't blame them in a way . . . they're not used to people like you . . ."

"You can't *blame* them! What's wrong with people like me?"

"Now don't you start. I'm telling you their opinion, not mine."

She felt she would explode. "You mean you're going along with this? You aren't going to tell them what I'm like, how you feel?"

"I didn't say I wasn't, but I need time. I can't do it all at once. My folks aren't as bad as you think. They want me to lead a normal life."

"What's not normal about liking a girl and wanting to paint?"

He shook his head. "You just don't get it. Listen. I'm going up to New Haven with the family for Christmas. Dad wants me to meet some of his pals at Yale. Maybe afterward . . ."

Once, she had lost some respect for Josh when he told her he was satisfied to take whatever he could get from his father's friends, but she pushed the recollection back so it would not become associated with Steve. Yet she could not control the cold anger in her voice.

"I hope you don't feel obliged to think what they think. I hope you don't feel it's *normal* to be an anti-Semite? Why can't you tell them they're way off course? You might be doing them a favor."

Steve ran his hands through his hair. "Man," he said, "life has been real easy on you. Everything is so simple. If Steve wants to paint, then Steve should paint. If Steve wants to knock his family off their pins by going steady with a Jewish girl, why, old Steve should do just that. Simple. Easy."

139

"I didn't say it was easy. I . . . I . . . just want you to try, not to give up. That is, if . . . if you really . . ."

His hands were on her shoulders and he drew her to him gently. "If what?" He whispered against her hair. "If I love you? Is that what you mean?"

She felt warm again. It was miraculous that words, no matter what they were, dissolved when Steve held her. The fact that he loved her was all that mattered; everything else would work out all right. She leaned her head against his shoulder. "Can we begin on New Year's, the way we planned?"

His shoulder tensed where her face leaned against it; there was a pause and then he began in a quiet, urging tone, "Debby, I just told you that I can't do it all at once. Anyway, there's something else . . ."

She sat up and faced him, but his eyes were fixed on the spokes of the steering wheel.

"My mother planned a New Year's Eve party. She sprang it on me this morning. She said it would be a good time to have my friends over, and an opportunity to make it up with Pat. Our families have been friends for—"

"I know, since before the *Mayflower*. How repulsively cozy!"

"Dammit, Debby."

"Well, it's true, isn't it? Isn't it repulsive how you want me to go on meeting you secretly, lying to my parents, slinking away with you after school so Pat Hamilton can call me names? And finally the joke is on me. She goes to your party and I stay home."

"Debby, please. Don't cry!" He turned away and looked out of the window, running his hands through his hair again in short, nervous strokes. "Maybe it isn't worth it," he said through clenched teeth.

These last words cut through her; she wanted to stop him before he could say any more. Let this not be the end, please; let it not be the end. But she had prodded Steve to the limit and this *was* the end. Where else could it go? It was over, and it was she who had pushed him to it.

"I'm sorry," he said. "But why does it have to be exactly on New Year's? I won't be back from New Haven until only a few days before then."

She was weak with relief. He was right when he said he needed time. She was putting as much pressure on him as were his parents or Pat Hamilton. She was the one who was wrong.

"Do you think I'm happy about the party, Deb? It's just something I have to go along with while I work things out, where you're concerned and about my being an artist—everything."

He reached inside his coat pocket and drew out a little box wrapped in gold paper. "Merry Christmas," he said, holding it out to her. "Or whatever that holiday is you celebrate—"

"Hanukkah," she said softly, staring at the box.

"Yeah. I guess that's it. Aren't you going to take it?"

141

"Oh, Steve," she said, reaching for the box and at the same time rummaging in her coat pocket for tissue to wipe her eyes.

When she unwrapped it finally, she opened the lid and lifted from its cotton cushion a gold chain bracelet with a single tiny heart hanging from one of the links.

"Oh! It's beautiful, Steve . . . it's just beautiful."

She put it around her wrist, but her fingers were so trembly he had to put it on for her. "Like it?" he whispered.

She could think of nothing meaningful to say; but when he kissed her, she wrapped her arms around him and held him close.

Later, at home, it was not until after dinner that she thought about not being able to wear the bracelet. The family would ask questions and she would have to lie again. She satisfied herself that there would be plenty of time to wear it afterward, when Steve had worked things out and they were together openly without fear. Then she would wear it always.

Yet, when she slid the bracelet to the bottom of her drawer and covered it over with handkerchiefs, she felt sneaky. Before meeting Steve, she had never hid anything from her family, and now she had done it twice; first with the portrait and now the bracelet. Don't dwell on such things, she cautioned herself. Do something, anything: biology, algebra . . . But she remembered she had a full two weeks in which to finish the assignments—two weeks that she had to fill without Steve. Don't dwell on that either, she added.

She found it near to claustrophobia to remain in her room, but the thought of socializing with the family was too grim.

While thumbing through the books on her desk she half-heartedly opened the volume of Bach exercises Mr. Stewart had given her—exercises that should better be called brain twisters, she told herself, but she continued to study them and, after a few moments of trying, to hum the score out loud. She got up with impulsive haste and went down to the piano.

She placed the book on the rack, sat down, and began to play. Then she stopped. Think. Organize, she said aloud, and continued to study the score for a while longer before she began to play again. The music was precise, exacting, yet pulsatingly beautiful. She felt the blood circulate in her arms, her wrists, and the stiffness went out of her fingers. She breathed deeply while she played, repeating passages over and over until she was satisfied.

Later, out of somewhere, Mother's voice called, "Debby! It's after ten o'clock. You've been playing almost two hours. It's time you stopped!"

She was exhausted when she crawled in between the cool sheets and sprawled over the bed letting her arms and legs go limp; experiencing a contentment inside her that was familiar, like the feeling she had once known through music and music alone. Tonight it had come

143

back to her and she wanted to lie awake and hold on, savor it, not let it slip away. She sighed deeply and within minutes, with no thoughts of anyone or anything, she was asleep.

If Steve's party was not enough to wreck Debby's vacation, Elly's calling to tell her that Josh had asked her to a formal dance was the final dab of gray to an already grim week. Of course, she told herself, she had no right to any sort of feelings about Elly's date; she had refused Josh two weeks earlier, believing she was to spend New Year's with Steve, and caring now that he had asked someone else made absolutely no sense. Josh was not the sort of person to sulk about things; he hadn't even sounded distraught at her refusal—oh, no, Josh would make the best of things as they were, no matter how he felt about them down deep. But how did he feel down deep? She had never been able to tell, not definitely anyway. His calm was a fence too high to jump, and too solidly picketed to see through. She remembered when they first met, her first week in North Haven; how his resemblance to Tony Mescuto had made her feel warm toward him right off. She still liked Josh, liked him as much as anyone she had ever known; but what she had looked for, hoped to find —a real resemblance to Tony—was simply not there. However, it was clear that Josh had given up on her too; she could imagine him putting his finger out to the air to see how the wind was blowing, then testing it further by asking her out for New Year's. When she refused he accepted the situation casually, moving on to more promising prospects. They would always be friends; Josh would never hold it against her—yet she wished now that it were she, instead of Elly, who was going out with Josh on New Year's Eve.

Three dismal days passed of helping Mother in the house, with only one evening with Madie to break the monotony. But Madie was going off with her family on a skiing trip, and the evening they spent together was all Madie pitched with excitement and Debby trying not to look or sound envious. The New Year loomed large and hideous and Debby had an excruciating picture of herself sitting at home with Grandpa while Mom and Dad went to their annual midnight movie. No doubt they would ask her to go along but she would rather be stretched on the rack than be seen at the North Haven Theater with her parents on New Year's Eve. How could she live through any evening knowing that Steve's party was in full swing? How did you get through things like that? How tough did you have to be—how full of anesthetics?

She brooded away another day and then, like manna from heaven, Mark called from Wisconsin to say he was bringing Stella home and Mother decreed that Debby was not to go anywhere on New Year's Eve because she was planning a family party. As though Mother didn't know she was dateless, but it proved that even Mother, at times, could be astute.

From the moment of Mark's phone call, Mrs. Rose began delegating jobs—from washing windows on the outside to chopping nuts for cookies and cakes. The house took on an atmosphere of preparation worthy of a crown prince and his bride, and even Debby found herself preoccupied with curiosity about her future sister-in-law. She might not know it, Debby told herself, but Stella had already won her eternal friendship by saving her from a New Year's Eve that promised the mood of an execution.

When finally the day came and the front door opened with Mark booming "Anybody home?" Mother virtually became air-borne and sailed out of the kitchen to greet them. Debby followed behind, hoping hard that Mother would not cry, that Dad would not say anything unpleasant, and that Grandpa for once would keep his epigrams to himself.

She caught sight of Stella as Mother embraced her, slim and almost as tall as Mark, and beautiful in an unusual way. Her skin was a deep ivory and her jet-black hair was pulled back into a chignon, adding to the Oriental air about her. She wore a simple black coat that looked far from new, but the red scarf around her neck heightened her color so that even the worn-out coat was attractive.

Dad's handshake was reserved, but Stella smiled at him, holding her head erect, demanding nothing more than he was willing to give.

Then Mark spotted Debby. "Hey," he said, pulling her into the circle, "since when are you the shrinking violet?"

Everyone laughed and talked at once and no one, until

146

minutes later, noticed Grandpa standing quietly, a little away from them, his eyes bright and the smile on his face warm and eager.

"Grandpa!" Mark said. "I knew there was something missing," and then he introduced Stella.

The two looked at each other, then Stella held out her hands and said to him in Hebrew, "*Shalom. Lee k'vod gadol ahdonee l'hakir at-chah.*" ("Revered Grandfather, I am greatly honored to meet you.")

Grandpa clasped her hands and embraced her. "*Shalom. Shalom,*" he answered. "*Baruch ha-ba-a.*" ("You bring us blessings.")

Dad coughed and Mother beckoned them into the dining room for a cup of tea before dinner. The large tears that had welled in Grandpa's eyes while greeting Stella in his beloved Hebrew language was more than any of them could bear.

All through dinner Debby watched Mark's face while he looked at his beautiful and tranquil Stella. He must be mad about her, she thought with a prick of envy. Stella was Mark's world now and somehow he no longer resembled the brother of old. Even his discussion of world events had an unfamiliar ring. Before, he would get terribly intense and often angry when Dad disagreed with him; but now he was willing to listen to Dad's opinions, even smile and concede a point or two. Oh, yes, he had certainly changed.

"What is your job like, Mark?" Dad asked, trying to sound casual.

"The Madison *Telegram,* Dad. I won't start there until I graduate in June, and then I'll be a junior reporter with fairly routine assignments at first." He looked at Stella and smiled. "But it will grow. I'm fairly confident of that."

Stella smiled back. It was obvious she shared Mark's confidence in himself and, moreover, had encouraged him.

"We are certainly sure of that," Stella said, and Debby repeated the sentence to herself in Stella's own accent. The way the r's came out, half-dropped, half-rolled, and the way she pronounced the word "that" intrigued her: We ahre cehrtenly sur-r-re of thet. It was a magnificent accent, not related to any one language but a Continental mixture that might have come from French or Italian or Hungarian, and it suited her dark exotic beauty so well.

"How much does the job pay?" Dad asked.

Mark and Stella grinned at each other.

"Fifty dollars a week, minus taxes," Mark said.

Dad's cheek twitched. "I'm not sure I see anything funny," he said. "It will cost almost as much to rent a decent apartment, unless of course you intend to live in a tree."

"Not a tree, but close to it," Mark said, still serene and smiling. "Friends of ours will be vacating a one-room apartment and have promised it to us. The rent is forty dollars a month and that includes hot plate and sink, and even a few luxuries like a bed that swings down from the wall and a table with two matching chairs."

"Not exactly a palace," Dad said.

148

Debby prayed that Dad would not lose his temper. But Mother interceded in time.

"When we were first married, we didn't have a palace either," she said—and Stella looked at her gratefully, speaking up with a catching eagerness.

"You must not worry for us," she said. "I am so happy to be in a family again. We promise not to give you any trouble." She could not have said anything more perfect, for after this simple but endearing statement the tone of the discussion changed abruptly.

When the two girls were alone before going to bed, Debby was determined to help Stella feel entirely comfortable. The evening had been dotted with awkward little silences that were not the fault of any one person except that Mother was busy in the kitchen for a long while, and Dad had apparently made up his mind that if he could not say anything pleasant he would remain silent. It was Grandpa who saved the evening by gently urging Stella to tell something about herself, and it whetted Debby's appetite for more.

When the two girls faced each other now in her room, Debby felt a sense of closeness, as though she had known Stella always. Stella had taken the pins out of her hair and it fell around her shoulders like a dark mantle.

"You have beautiful hair, Stella."

"I like yours better," Stella answered, and then she laughed. "People are never satisfied, are they?"

"I suppose not." She hesitated for a moment. "Stella, maybe you don't want to talk about it any more . . .

149

But how does anyone live through what you did? I mean
. . . well, having your parents taken away to a concentration camp while you got carted off to strangers?"

"But I was just a baby at the time. When I was rescued
by the underground in Hungary and smuggled out to a
convent in France, I was not even aware that my parents
had been killed. I grew to be four years old without
knowledge of parents or what it meant to have such
things. All I knew of love was the feel of the nun's robe
against my face."

"Were you afraid?"

Stella sighed. "There were times, Deborah," she said
after a long moment, "when I was so frightened I wanted
to hide behind anything that could give me shelter. After
the war the Jewish Agency took me from the convent and
sent me to a Children's Village in Israel. I was frightened
then because there were no flowing robes and hushed
gentle voices; instead, there were singing and dancing
and roughhousing and playing, and all I could do was
cling to my teacher's hand. It did not matter to me if I
were left out of games, or even whether I received my
food, so long as my teacher's hand was close to mine."

"Did you ever remember your mother?" Debby asked
softly.

"No, but I had made up a picture in my mind of what
my mother might have looked like; and I used to search
the faces of all the women who worked at the Village,
trying to fit this face or that face to the image I had of my
mother. I decided, finally, that my teacher's face was like

that of my mother and thereafter I never left her side. When she married and left the Children's Village it was almost a week before the others could get me to take food. I very nearly died."

"How terrible!" Debby whispered. "I feel ashamed how people, myself included, stew over nothing. You know something, Stella? I thought I was going to die— because, well, because I didn't have a date on New Year's. Can you believe that? I hope you won't laugh."

Stella fixed her large dark eyes on Debby's face. "How could I laugh?" she asked gently. "Loneliness is a bad thing no matter how it comes to us. When my great-aunt from Wisconsin came to Israel and took me from the Children's Village to this country, I should have been the happiest and most grateful girl alive. But I was not. I was lonely for many years afterward. Then, the year I entered the university my great-aunt died and I was alone again."

"Oh, how could you go on after so much?"

"What was I to do? I had to find a place for myself, since I had no other relatives. I was frightened again and I wanted to pack my things and run; but of course I had no place to go, so I got a job in the library at the university and went to school at night. After a while my fea turned into mere loneliness, then suddenly—I don't know why—I felt stronger inside."

"Do you think it always happens that way—that things just seem to jell?"

"I don't know. Perhaps it is the process of becoming a

person. With me, it was giving my fear a chance to go away until I found—"

"Until you found someone like Mark?"

Stella flushed and looked down at her fingers. "Yes . . . I suppose that's right."

"I'm glad you found him, Stella. He's lucky. It took him a while to become a person too—and don't think any of us were too optimistic about it."

Stella looked up from scrutinizing her fingers and met Debby's eyes frankly. "Tell me," she said, "what is it that frightens you so?"

"Me? Wh-what makes you think that?"

"Oh, perhaps I am wrong; but I seem to feel it in you . . . and your eyes are very troubled."

"Are they? I can't imagine why . . . really." Then for a wild moment she wanted to tell Stella everything: the hopelessness she felt about her music, the dizzying confusion where Steve was concerned, the aimless and willy-nilly road she felt herself traveling. But when she met Stella's eyes they were too direct, too frank, and she could only look away again with embarrassment that was almost shame. "I suppose everyone is afraid of some things," she said.

"Oh, yes," Stella agreed. "That is true enough." Then, as though sensing Deborah's reluctance, she smiled broadly and changed the subject. "I'm so anxious to hear you play the piano, Deborah. Imagine how it pleases me to come back to a family of musicians."

Debby looked at her curiously.

"Yes . . . yes," Stella continued, her black eyes shining. "My mother and father were musicians in Budapest before the Nazis came. The nuns told me that my mother was acclaimed the finest pianist in all Hungary. And now I am to have a sister who will be the same!"

"I wouldn't count on that," Debby answered wistfully.

"But why? Mark tells me you have great talent."

"Oh, yes, great talent—no luck."

"Do not speak of luck," Stella said. "I was born to misfortune, and see me now! The happiest girl in all America!"

Stella's face was alive and vibrant with happiness, and Debby had the sudden impulse to share something deeper—something intimate. If she could not tell Stella everything, at least she could go halfway. She hopped off the bed, went to the closet, and took the painting out from behind her clothes. When she held it out to Stella her hands were trembling, but she managed to smile. "How do you like it?" she asked.

Stella studied it for a moment. "Did you paint it?" she asked.

"Oh, no. A . . . a friend of mine did though."

"Is it supposed to be you?"

"Why, yes . . . doesn't it—"

"Look like you?" Stella studied it some more. "In some ways it does, but not really. You have more strength than the girl in this picture . . . more pride . . . no, that is not you."

Debby withdrew it quickly and shoved it into the

153

closet again. She came back to the bed where Stella was sitting and made an effort to yawn. "I don't know why I pulled that out," she said. "I guess I wanted someone's opinion. I've never shown it to anyone before."

Stella did not say any more and Deborah snapped off the light.

When the room was quiet, Stella called to her from the other twin bed. "It doesn't matter, Debby," she said softly, "if the picture looks like you or not. It is a good painting and it seems that the artist who painted it was unhappy inside himself. If someday he should change, he would see you differently—as I do."

Debby whispered back good night; but she lay there for a long time, staring into the darkness. If she truly had more strength, more pride than the girl in the picture, then why wasn't she able to show it? Either she *was* the girl in the painting or she was not. And how, oh, how, did you know?

Twelve

Steve's visit to New Haven seemed to have strengthened his feelings that he and Debby should keep their meetings hidden for at least a few weeks longer. Debby told herself that a few weeks were nothing compared to her love for him; but lately, after walking four blocks after school to meet him on an out-of-the-way street, and then shivering in the car, she began to doubt. A sense of restlessness and impatience took hold of her. She never imagined it would be so difficult to manage a secret love affair, guarding against a slip of the tongue or a reaction at the lunch table when Steve's name was mentioned. If Elly or Josh, or Madie Weeks, with whom she had become quite close and who knew Pat Hamilton well, looked at her in anything but a perfectly casual manner she worried lest they suspected something.

At home she had to reassure herself constantly that the portrait remained undiscovered in the back of her closet, and the bracelet at the bottom of her handkerchief drawer. When Mother wanted to clean her closet she had virtually jumped at her—and Mother had stood back, startled. "My goodness," she had said, "you would think there was gold hidden there!" And Debby found herself snapping back, "What if there is! It's my room, isn't it?" Apologies followed, then forgiveness, and finally a nagging humiliation inside herself for everything that was happening.

Jessie's audition was an anxiety that grew daily; evenings had to be used for the increasing load of homework and term papers; school hours were crammed full, especially now that Madie had chosen her to be assistant decorations chairman for the senior dance; and after school, when she might have practiced, she saw Steve instead.

Mr. Stewart had not spared her the one time she had gone back to play for him after the Christmas vacation.

"How many more weeks do you have until the audition?" he asked her.

"Three, I think, but I'll practice harder—"

"You'll have to, young lady—I should say you will!"

She had not gone back to him since, and now the audition was only two weeks away. She had to do something now—today.

She was late meeting Steve and, when he opened the door of the car for her, he looked at his watch. "I thought you weren't coming," he said.

"Elly caught me at my locker," she answered glumly. "I had to listen while she raved about her dates with Josh."

"There's something about that girl," Steve said, "that reminds me of Angie Kress. They're both sort of cheesy."

"Oh, I don't know. At least Elly isn't vicious. And why shouldn't she rave about her dates? She has a good time."

"Hey, you're the one who brought it up."

"Well, maybe I shouldn't have. What's wrong with having fun? Seems as though everyone does, but me."

"So that's it."

"What?"

"You're sore about meeting me like this."

"Why shouldn't I be sore? While other people are having fun, I'll end up with frostbite or pneumonia. Maybe we should go to the Arctic and make love on a glacier? We seem to be headed that way."

He reached out for her hand, but she pulled away from him. In her abrupt turning she caught the expression on his face and said, "I'm sorry, Steve." Then, looking down at her fingers, she muttered, "I'll bet I apologize to one person or another a dozen times a day. I should have a record made."

"Listen, Deb," he said. "I've decided to have it out with my folks about you and law school and everything that matters to me. I didn't tell you before, but they got me into a kind of trap in New Haven introducing me to everyone as though it were all settled. I was miserable, yet I didn't know what to do except let things ride for a while; but I know now I couldn't study anything but art. I want to go to the Art Institute right here in Chicago.

157

I'm one of those people who shouldn't go to college; they'll just have to understand that."

"Oh, Steve, I'm so glad! But it's only right, because your talent deserves it; you'll see, they'll appreciate you at the Art Institute and I'll bet your parents will encourage you too. Tell them today. Right after you leave me. Then I'll be able to . . ."

He smiled. "Not right today." He interrupted. "In a few weeks."

"A few weeks! But why? Why put it off again? You said yourself you—"

"I have to think out the angle, that's all."

"Can't you tell them straight out, honestly? Does there have to be an angle?"

"You don't know my father. He's a lawyer, remember? He can make anybody's arguments look like something out of a comic strip; anyway, he's been jumpy as the devil about a case. When it's all over, in a couple of weeks, I'll talk to him about us and the Art Institute and everything that needs to be hashed out; I promise, Deb. It's not only for you; it's for me too."

She studied the half-moons of her fingernails. A few weeks in this cold car were infinity, but she had to stand by him now. She had helped him, urged him to this decision and, whether she wanted to be or not, she was part of it. Yet the issue of her practicing had to be settled before she became enmeshed deeper and deeper.

"What do we do in the meantime?" she asked.

"We wait. Just like before. You want to, don't you? It's worth it to you, isn't it?"

"Steve, I—I can't. I mean I really have to practice. Jessie's counting on me and Mr. Stewart's been so nice."

He slapped his hand to his head and whistled. "Man, if that's not like a woman! The last time you talked about Stewart you were a candidate for the homicide squad; now, suddenly, he's the great white father."

"I don't like him at all—that is, I really hate him—but he's very helpful and—oh, I don't know any more."

Neither of them spoke for a moment, but she finally broke the silence. "Steve? Don't you think it would be a good idea not to see each other until . . . well, until after you've talked to your parents? And in the meantime I'll practice, and after the audition we'll both be free and can start over the way it should be. Steve, I just have to practice. And you can paint in the meantime. You haven't been doing much painting lately; it would be good for you, really it would."

She stopped for breath. "It's not that I don't want to wait, or that I don't think it's worth it. I just have to practice, Steve; honest to goodness I have to practice."

He did not answer and they sat there looking at each other—she feeling that something had changed; not knowing whether it was within herself or in him, but she could feel it hurt. Then, as though he too had detected something and was equally alarmed, he reached out and pulled her to him. "Okay," he whispered. "You practice and I'll paint." He held her very close while he spoke quietly and urgently.

"When I was at Yale I imagined never smelling paint again, and I saw myself in the center of a stack of law-

159

books piled so high I couldn't see over or around them. And then I missed you and decided to tell them about us, whatever they thought or did." He brushed her hair with his lips. "I love you, Debby. I love you more than you think."

Two days before the audition, Debby got permission to miss two days of school so she could go to the South Side for rehearsals. Mr. Mason had been working with Jessie until now, and he had said that two days would be sufficient for the two of them to synchronize their roles; that is, if she knew the music well.

While she put the few final things into her suitcase she thought to herself that it was because of Mr. Stewart that she knew the music as well as she did and could feel entirely confident. She smiled to herself. Who would have believed that she would ever feel anything like gratitude to Mr. Stewart?

Just before leaving her room she stopped, went to her drawer and drew out the bracelet from underneath the pile of handkerchiefs. She held it to her cheek and felt the smooth, cool metal prick the warmth of her skin; then, on impulse, she slipped it into her purse.

Dad was waiting to take her to the train and, as she had anticipated, Mother had packed her a sandwich.

"But I'll only be on the train for an hour," she said.

"Take it," Mother insisted. "You might not have a big enough dinner tonight."

"Why not? Mrs. Perkins is a terrific cook."

"I didn't say she couldn't cook, Debby. They're poor people."

"They eat," she said, and stopped herself. This was no time to quarrel with Mother.

"I didn't say they didn't eat, either. I simply said they're poor people, and I'm not sure you should burden them for three days. Why don't you stay with Midge?"

Dad interrupted. "Do they have enough sleeping space? After all, they have six children."

"I suppose they do," she answered. "If they didn't, they wouldn't have asked me."

Dad ignored her statement. "Negro families double up and don't mind it. You aren't used to that kind of living, Debby."

She pulled her gloves on with short, staccato motions. "Talk about prejudice!" she breathed. "Just because they're Negroes, does it have to mean they live in a pit? I've been there lots of times. It's a *nice* home."

"Debby!" Mother said indignantly. "Who ever said it wasn't? I said they were poor and Mrs. Perkins might not want to refuse you."

"Oh, Mother . . ." she began again, but Mother's arms were around her now.

"Never mind," she said. "Good luck, dear. I'm really proud of you. I know how hard it has been." And then, of all the wacky things, Mother was crying.

At the station Dad kissed her good-by, wished her luck, and told her to call home every evening. Then, just before she got on the train, he took her hands and held them in his. "Debby, darling," he said, "your chance will come too. You're a straight-shooting girl, and I'm proud of you."

She kissed him quickly and turned into the train. A moment later, in her seat by the window, she watched the North Haven Station slide back behind her, then the printing plant and the bowling alleys, and, more rapidly, the large supermarket and skating rink. She stared out of the window for a long while and then reached into her purse for a tissue. Her fingers caught on a link of the bracelet and she lifted it out. She laid it across her wrist and was starting to fasten the clasp when her father's words came back to her: "You're a straight-shooting girl, and I'm proud of you." She slipped the bracelet off quickly and dropped it into her purse again. There was a hollowness inside her like a dark, gaping canyon.

The next morning Deborah sat up sleepily on the day bed in Jessie's room. Jessie and her sister Margaret were fast asleep in the double bed next to it, and in the corner of the room three-year-old Ethalyn was standing up in her crib leaning against the rails with her finger in her mouth, watching. Deborah smiled at Ethalyn. For the two days she had been at the Perkinses', Ethalyn had kept a quiet surveillance, her round black eyes following, her head turning slowly to watch Deborah's every move.

Debby crawled out of the day bed, tiptoed over to the crib, and cupped Ethalyn's small face in her hands.

"You don't miss a thing, do you, baby?"

Ethalyn's eyes rolled to see the tips of Debby's fingers on her face, but she said nothing.

"Guess what?" Debby said. "When I get home I'm going to buy you a present. What would you like? A dolly? A new dress? A picture book, maybe?"

Ethalyn's face remained stoic.

"Well, then," Debby continued, "how about, let's see, a great big old Teddy bear to sleep with? You can put him right here in your bed and hug him at night, like this." She lifted Ethalyn out of her crib and held her close for a moment. Ethalyn blinked her eyes.

"How about that Teddy bear?" Debby asked her, and Ethalyn blinked again. "Then give me a kiss. Right here." Ethalyn stared for a moment before planting a tiny wisp of a kiss on Debby's cheek.

Jessie was awake now and came over to them. "Come on," she said sleepily to Ethalyn, "I'd better get you to the bathroom."

When Debby and Jessie were dressed, Mrs. Perkins sat them down at the kitchen table for breakfast. The kitchen was the largest room in the five-room apartment, and in the center of it was a dining-room table that seated ten persons comfortably. Mrs. Perkins had the table set with ruby glass plates and cups for just the two of them. Mr. Perkins and the three boys, all older than Jessie, had already left for work and Ethalyn had been fed breakfast with her father. Margaret was still asleep.

"I don't know why you won't eat just something," Mrs.

163

Perkins said to Jessie. "If you're planning on singing this morning, you'd best get yourself some energy to hold you up. I'm not asking you to eat Christmas dinner; I mean just something."

"Momma . . . please . . ." Jessie begged.

"Your mother's right," Debby said, feeling too nervous herself to eat but pretending for Jessie's sake. She had lain awake half the night and had heard Jessie tossing in her bed, moaning now and then. She had imagined Jessie crying and wanted to get up and talk to her, but Margaret and Ethalyn were asleep and she was afraid she might awaken them.

Mrs. Perkins filled Debby's cup with hot chocolate and put three flapjacks on her plate. She did the same for Jessie.

"I'm going to sit here till you eat it," she said to both girls, settling her large frame in a chair beside them. She pushed the butter, syrup, and jelly closer to them and sat there waiting.

"I'll eat just one," Jessie said. "It's not good for my voice—"

"Don't worry so much," Debby said. "It will be beautiful; you'll see. We had a perfect run-through last night."

Jessie was close to tears; she picked at a flapjack with her fork but seemed lost in thought.

Mrs. Perkins reached out for her daughter's hand. "Did you say your prayers last night?" she asked her solemnly. Jessie nodded. "Then what's all this heavy worrying about? Don't you think the Lord knows how you feel?

Now you look at your Momma." She smiled a broad, white-toothed smile and her large dark face was bright with happiness. "Your Momma did some praying too, and she hasn't a one bit of worry left."

When breakfast was over, Mrs. Perkins fussed over them, seeing they were properly buttoned up, gloved, and scarved before leaving.

She kissed Jessie and squeezed Debby's hand. "You're a mighty fine young woman, Deborah." Her face was serious and a bit sad when she said it, but in a moment her expression changed to joviality once more. "Poppa's bringing home a turkey this morning and we're going to have the biggest feast this family's ever laid eyes on, for Jessie and this sweet gal here. We're going to do a heap of celebrating."

Jessie was mournful. "How do you know there'll be anything to celebrate?"

"Listen to the girl talk," Mrs. Perkins said. "I know, that's all. I know."

While walking down the four flights of the apartment building, Debby marveled at Mrs. Perkins; why, she acted as though she *did* know. There wasn't the least bit of doubt in her mind.

When they were a block from Purcell High School, Debby began to feel queasy in her stomach. She shouldn't have eaten those flapjacks, she told herself, but down deep she knew it was not the flapjacks. The trouble was going back to Purcell again, facing the auditions that should rightly have been hers. She felt a wave of nausea

165

come over her, and she was convinced she could not go through with it. Mr. Mason would take over, and it might even be better for Jessie if he would. Oh, how did she get here anyway? Why had she let herself in for this agony? The Purcell scholarship belonged to her and to no one else. She had worked for years, slaved over the piano, studied music theory when other kids were having fun. Jessie had not worked nearly as hard as she had. Jessie had spent her time fooling around at the Settlement House. It wasn't right; it wasn't fair. She felt too nauseous to play at all, let alone for something as important as this. She would tell Mr. Mason, and Jessie would have to understand; but it made no difference even if she didn't.

Just before entering the building, Jessie stopped. She looked ill.

"Debby," she said in a hoarse, faint voice, "I can't. I just can't."

Debby looked at Jessie's drawn, anxious face for a long moment, and then she swallowed back her own nausea. "I know how you feel," she said. "Come on. You'll be all right when you see Mr. Mason."

In the front row of the empty auditorium three well-dressed men sat quietly. Mr. Mason took a seat next to the oldest of the three, a short, white-haired man with a pale, flaccid face.

Mr. Mason signaled to them, in the wings, and the girls came out to the grand piano on the stage. Debby arranged the music carefully on the rack, adjusted herself to the stool, and waited until Jessie was ready. Then she looked at the music and scanned the first measures, establishing the tempo and key firmly in her mind before putting her fingers on the keys. Jessie straightened her shoulders. The reels of the tape recorder began to spin and Debby played the first chords. She continued the introduction, gave Jessie the cue, and then her accompaniment receded into the background while Jessie's powerful contralto voice rose above it and filled the auditorium with glorious sound. It proceeded without a flaw; Jessie's voice was beautiful, brilliant.

When the Bach was finished, Jessie stood quietly, her head lowered, while Debby arranged the music for the spiritual as quietly as possible so the tape recorder would not pick up any needless noises. She played the short introduction and Jessie lifted her head and began again as though she were singing in church, her whole body erect, her hands clasped in front of her, a luster of serenity and joy emanating from her face.

"Every time I feel the spirit . . . moving in my heart, I will pray. . . ."

Debby glanced from the piano to the men sitting in the front row; the expression on their faces was obviously that of interest and approval. The man with white hair turned to Mr. Mason and smiled.

When it was over, the applause was hearty and Jessie bowed her head. Then, as Debby got up from her seat, Jessie turned to the piano, smiled brilliantly, and applauded her. The three men followed suit and Mr. Mason's glowing face might have lighted the auditorium on its own power.

Debby stood off to the side while Jessie was congratulated by the judges, who asked her questions and smiled when her excitement was apparent in half-stammered answers. Debby stood there clutching the music tightly, wondering if it would not be proper for her to leave. They wanted to talk to Jessie, not her. She had fulfilled her obligation and she was no longer needed; this was Jessie's moment and her own part in it was minor, secondary. Once it might have been hers, but there was no point in hoping any longer. The Purcell auditions were over.

She felt a hand on her shoulder, and turned around to Mr. Mason standing beside her, his soft, sensitive eyes looking directly into hers. "You're a true musician," he said. "If I ever doubted it, now I'm sure. It required a special kind of discipline to go through with this."

She could not answer him and tried instead to blink back the too ready tears that were starting in her eyes.

"Have you convinced yourself?" he asked her.

"I don't know . . ."

"Yes, you do, Debby, or you wouldn't be here." He looked over his shoulder to where the judges stood with Jessie. "Dr. Samuel," he called, "can I see you a moment?"

The short, white-haired man nodded congenially and came over to them.

"This is Dr. Isaac Samuel, Deborah. He's a professor

at the New York Academy of Music. He's also on the staff of Juilliard."

"How do you do, young lady," Dr. Samuel said. "You did a nice job . . ."

Mr. Mason approved his remark by nodding, and said in rapid succession, "I wonder if you might have time to hear a little more, Dr. Samuel? Deborah's been a student of mine for a long time. She would have been competing for this scholarship if she hadn't moved to another school district. She's up in North Haven now with Mr. Stewart."

"Is that so?" Dr. Samuel said, looking at his watch. "I know Jim Stewart very well. Excellent man."

She held fast to the book of music in her hands, her eyes fixed on Dr. Samuel's snowy hair that was glaringly bright under the bare illumination of the auditorium. His small, round form seemed to expand and take in her entire field of vision; she stared at him in answer to his slow smile.

"I'd like to hear the young lady play again," he said. "But I'm due at Northwestern University in about an hour, which makes me a little late right now."

"That's too bad," Mr. Mason said. "I had hoped—"

"I'm sorry too," Dr. Samuel answered. "Some other time perhaps. I'll be back at Northwestern in late April, and maybe then . . ."

He held his hand out to Mr. Mason, who thanked him for coming to Purcell and said he hoped to hear about Jessie soon.

Debby mumbled good-by automatically and stood there feeling like a mechanical toy whose spring had lost its tautness, telling herself that nothing had been lost or gained. If she did not think about it, she could pretend that the conversation between Mr. Mason and Dr. Samuel had never occurred. She had to make herself believe that, or this roller coaster of hope and despair would tear her to shreds. Don't care about it, she thought, don't care. But every word she told herself was like a dull, reverberating thud.

When Dr. Samuel was gone, Mr. Mason turned to her once more, his face obviously downcast. "You seem destined to travel the rocky road, Deborah. I don't know what to say, except that you've won my respect by coming down here. You're going to make it someday, you know; you played beautifully. You never played Bach for me like that—Mr. Stewart up there in North Haven must have something I don't."

"I don't think so . . ." she told him; but the idea took hold, and she thought suddenly that Mr. Stewart might have arranged things differently. She could not help believing, even though her affection for Mr. Mason wanted to crowd out the thoughts, that in the same situation Mr. Stewart would have arranged things so that Dr. Samuel would have had time to hear her play.

The party at Midge's house was in full swing when she and Jessie arrived. They were late because the dinner Mrs. Perkins cooked—turkey with all the fixin's, as she put it—had stuffed them so full they could hardly budge. Ethalyn, for the first time, had sat on Debby's lap without trying to squirm off and had whispered the single words "Teddy bear" in her ear. She had whispered back "Just as soon as I get home," and Ethalyn was now solidly imbued with love. Jessie's nerves were considerably soothed after the turkey dinner and she said that if it weren't for Debby she'd fall right into bed instead of going to the party; but when Debby falteringly offered to stay home too, Jessie laughed. "Are you kidding?" she said.

Midge had invited all of the old gang to the party, and, when they walked in, Debby and Jessie were fallen upon, kissed, asked if the results to the audition were known yet, and whisked into the living room with their coats half off.

"Hey, wait a minute," Midge said. "Let them get their coats off. For goodness' sakes, someone would think you'd never seen celebrities before."

Midge took their coats into the bedroom while at the same moment the apartment buzzer went off again. "Get it, will you, Deb?" Midge called. Debby pressed the buzzer that unlocked the downstairs door of the apartment house, then opened the hall door to wait. Tony Mescuto was taking the stairs three at a time and, when he saw her, he put his guitar case down, lifted her off her feet, and kissed her solidly.

"Tony, Tony," she gasped, out of breath. "It's so good to see you."

"Baby," he said, "you are balm to the eyes, sweet scent to the nose, and honey to the lips."

She poked him. "Same old nut. Come on in— Hey, are we going to get serenaded tonight?" she asked, looking at the guitar case. "You haven't played that thing for ages. Or did you get inspired when I left?"

"Baby, all I've done since you left was play the blues, melancholy blues."

"Oh, sure," she laughed while Tony meandered into the living room. Debby watched him for a moment while he walked toward the others, wondering how she had ever thought that Josh Sandow resembled him. They had the same coloring, but aside from that there was nothing alike in the two boys.

Within minutes after Tony's arrival the party was in full swing. Debby played hot jazz on Midge's piano, and she and Jessie took turns improvising the bass while the other played the treble. Midge, Tony, Andrea, Sophie, Bill Bramson, and Binky Jones hung over the piano, snapping their fingers, clapping, moving their shoulders, and beating time with their feet. Jessie sang a couple of blues numbers and they all said she sounded exactly like Ella Fitzgerald. Midge told her she was crazy to go for opera when she had a blues voice like that; and Jessie laughed, answering that the part about her being crazy was probably true.

Midge served turkey sandwiches and Jessie blinked mischievously at Debby when they each were handed a plateful with Coke and chocolate cake to go with it.

172

Debby toasted Jessie with her sandwiches. "Bottoms up," she said while Jessie took a deep breath and bit into her sandwich half-heartedly.

After the food Tony took out his guitar. Everyone was sprawled lazily now and Midge doused all but one small light. She brought a stool from the kitchen and Tony perched on it, his guitar braced against his knee. His baritone swept softly through the room against the background of chords from the guitar. "I dreamt I saw Joe Hill last night as live as he could be."

Debby sat back in the shadows watching the gangly outline of Tony Mescuto bent over his guitar with the dim light subtly playing around his face and the sound of his husky voice filling the room. Lazily she recalled conversation earlier in the evening.

"I hear you've got a scholarship to the University of Chicago, Tony," Bill Bramson had said.

"Yep. But they made me promise to stay away from the beatniks, keep my hair cut, and all that. But what they don't know is that I'm the precise opposite to the beatnik; I wanna live, man, I wanna live."

"Tony's going to be a ward healer. At the University of Chicago they call it political science. Tony's going to change the world, didn't you poor people know that?"

Tony's slow smile began. "I'm gonna try, baby. I'm gonna try."

Watching him now, his eyes half closed and his body swaying slightly while he sang his sad song about Joe Hill, she knew that, in spite of what anyone said or

173

joked about, Tony Mescuto, like Mark, *would* try to change the world. How wonderful and exciting it was going to be for the girl who would share it with him, like Stella and Mark in their one room, holding on and believing in each other without fancy family props. Oh, there had to be more to living than turning yourself into a piece of tracing paper so you could be an exact copy of what went before you. Why couldn't Steve see that? Why was he so afraid? And Josh. Maybe he did want to be a doctor, but did he have to go about it in precisely the same way his father had? Her thoughts jumped back to Steve again and she realized she had not worn the bracelet in the three days she had been away from home. She had meant to show it to Jessie and Midge, tell them everything; but something had held her back. Now she was glad she hadn't; she could not figure out exactly why, but she was glad.

Tony was strumming the guitar faster now and beginning another song while motioning for them all to join in. She sat back in her chair, took a breath, and began to sing, "There was an old lady who swallowed a fly . . . I don't know why she swallowed the fly." . . .

Thirteen

Mr. Stewart called Debby to his office on the Monday morning after she got back from her week end at Jessie's. As usual he was immured in his chair at the desk, solemn-looking in the gray suit with the jacket all buttoned up as though he were a mannequin and the clothes had been fitted and tucked and pressed after they were on him. Still, despite his trim and businesslike appearance, he looked different.

Before, he had seemed cold and aloof; but now he appeared quietly contemplative. She had once judged him as uninteresting and harsh, but she regarded him now as a conscientious man with no time for dilettantes. She could not account for the change, but she could pinpoint the precise moment when her image of him had turnstiled in her mind. Standing in the auditorium next to Mr. Mason, she had realized with a peculiar certainty that Mr. Stewart would have arranged things so that the important man from New York would have heard her play. She had not gotten over the feeling that Mr. Mason had let her down at the crucial moment—although it was painful to believe that of him now, because once she had thought of him as the epitome of musicians; of all artists, in fact. She had built stories around him: about his being hungry and refusing to sell his music books in order to buy food, or giving up a promising career of his own so he might continue teaching at Purcell High School.

Mr. Mason's faults, she had believed, were also his virtues. If he were absent-minded and disheveled, it was because he cared for nothing but music; and if he closed his ears to mistakes occasionally, it was because he did not want to discourage her. Alongside Mr. Mason she had considered Mr. Stewart an impostor, comically miscast, more suited to teaching bookkeeping than music. Yet it had turned out that, for all of his tactlessness and picayune efficiency, Mr. Stewart had been able to extract a quality of performance that Mr. Mason was never able to get from her. What accounted for the difference? She could not say; she knew only that it was unsettling to like one person, to respect another—with the two feelings separate and seemingly unrelated.

She sat down next to his desk without being invited, waiting until he finished sorting some papers. There was a form in front of him that looked like an application blank, and he began to write on it. Then he looked up.

"What's your address, Miss Rose?"

"I beg your pardon?"

"Your address," he repeated. "You do know it, don't you?"

176

"Uh . . . seven forty-one Elm Street."

"Your birthday?"

"July fifth. I'll be eighteen then."

"Your father's name and occupation?"

"Nathan Rose, pharmacist." She was consumed with curiosity. How could he calmly sit there asking questions without explaining? It was stupid of him—well, typical anyway. A glimmer of the old irritation returned, and she decided to speak up.

"What's it all about? Shouldn't I know?"

"I suppose you should," he answered, "when I'm finished here. Is your mother employed? What is her first name?"

"Sylvia, and she helps Dad in the store. Gee, Mr. Stewart, can't you tell me?"

"Employed part time," he muttered, while writing.

Darn him anyway, she thought. Why did he have to spoil things just as she was beginning to consider him human.

"Any brothers or sisters?" he continued. "If so, their names and occupations, please."

"One brother, Mark. He's a student, and about to be married."

"Who pays his tuition?"

She hesitated before answering. What nerve! Who did he think he was, asking personal family questions without even telling her what it was all about? She toyed with the possibility of not telling him; but she felt his eyes on her, waiting.

"My . . . father, I guess. But Mark had partial scholarships and worked on his own. My father couldn't afford all of it."

Mr. Stewart grunted. "Where does he go to school?"

She felt like clawing him, but she concentrated on getting a tissue out of her purse while she mumbled, "University of Wisconsin."

"All right," he said, with a note of finality. "The rest you do yourself. Take a moment or two to think, and then write on this paper."

She took the blank sheet he held out and put it in her lap. What was she supposed to think about? Had the man suddenly gone berserk? She waited until he put another few words on the form and then she looked at him directly, hoping he would get the message that she was utterly bewildered.

"You are to write," he said, his eyes meeting hers, "why you believe you should have a scholarship in music at Northwestern University."

She felt a sudden chill as though a wave had crashed over her. She averted her eyes quickly and looked down at the blank white paper in her lap. She stared at it, and its whiteness glared back as though it defied her to transform its lifelessness into an instrument that might bring her all that she had hoped for.

"What's the matter, Deborah?" she heard him say. He had never before called her by her given name, and hearing it spoken gently now, like the last block placed on a tall and wobbling tower, was more than she could endure. She held her breath to control herself, but the sob came out of her throat as though it had been yanked out like a tooth.

He made no move to stop her from crying; he merely sat there, waiting while she regained her composure.

"I can't," she whispered finally.

"You can't what?" He asked.

"I can't try again. Every time I get close, something goes wrong, like my chess games with Mark and Grandpa; when it comes to making a checkmate, I can't do it. No matter how I try, there's always a false move somewhere —a slip at the very last minute to stop me. I've stopped playing chess; I hate the game now."

"You think music is like chess?"

"Maybe not. But success is. No matter how hard you try, no matter how well you know the moves, there's the element of luck—plain luck. I don't seem to have it. I never have, I guess."

"Nonsense." Mr. Stewart's voice rang in its familiar impatient tone. "The reason you never made a checkmate is the same reason you're not willing to take another crack at a scholarship. You're more intrigued with feeling sorry for yourself than you are with work; you're afraid to examine the false moves, the slips, and the errors, and you're too lazy to study them and work them through. Isn't that more like it?"

He got up from his chair and went to the cupboard, where he lifted a tape recorder off the shelf and set it down on a table. "These are my secrets," he said, while

179

adjusting a reel of tape to the instrument. He motioned to her to keep her seat and then, after turning a switch, he sat down too.

She had expected to hear a recorded lecture and she started when piano music filled the room, a halfhearted, hesitating rendition of the Bach oratorio she had played for him when she came to ask for help. She recognized it by the three starts she had made. Why, that was the time, after the piece was finally under way, when she had been so pleased and cocksure about her playing. She had even considered Mr. Stewart nervy and downright contrary when he suggested she study with him and practice exercises before trying the number again. Was this how it had really sounded? The tempo was off; the phrasing was wild and the notes were jammed together in some spots while in others the pauses and hesitations were unbearable.

She felt the color rise to her face and she prayed he would shut the thing off; after an agony of moments, he did. "I'm—I'm ashamed," she murmured.

He smiled at her. "All right," he said. "Now you can hear it the way it should be played."

He switched the instrument on again; the reel spun for a moment and then she heard the music. She sat back and shut her eyes. The melody flowed in tempo and the precise countertheme fulfilled its exquisite harmony. There was a combination of mind and heart in this music that was unsurpassable; it was all strength and yet it was all beauty. She felt the tears start to her eyes again and a constricting ache of envy. She did not want to listen any

180

more; she wanted to get out of here—get home where she could start practicing again, lose herself in work for hours, days, and nights. If hard work was the necessary companion to talent, then she was prepared; she would do anything to obliterate the mess she had once proudly exhibited. Luck did not make the difference between the first rendition and the second; it was she herself who was sitting in judgment, and the first performer would not go far with her. But the second—oh, that was the one who came through with skill, discipline, and honesty and not by chance or bluff or defiance.

"Well?" Mr. Stewart asked. "Did you like this better?"

"It makes me jealous," she said. "I wish . . . oh, I'd give anything . . ."

Laughing heartily, he interrupted her. "Oh, would you now?" And then he switched off the tape recorder. "That last version," he said, still smiling, "was played by an obstinate but talented girl who, for once in her life, examined the errors."

The way he said it and the way he looked at her—She gasped. "Oh, no! Was that *me?*"

He nodded and went past her to his desk with the usual brusqueness. "I'm optimistic," he said, in passing, "about your getting the scholarship. A close friend of mine from New York, a Dr. Samuel, phoned the same day he heard you play at Purcell; he was very impressed with you and sorry he didn't have time to hear more of your work. But he'll be at Northwestern again in the spring; he's on their auditions board too."

She had hardly heard him, she was so lost in the deli-

181

cious knowledge that it was actually she who had played the second time. It was like a coronation at the moment of being crowned.

"I can't believe it," she muttered, getting up from her chair. "Was it really me? It doesn't seem possible. I—"

"Yes, it was you," Mr. Stewart said matter-of-factly. "That is, you, after you stopped sulking and buckled down to work. Sit down, Deborah."

He picked up a pencil and began to turn it over in his hands as though he had to be careful about what he planned to say. "I once knew a young man," he began slowly, "and he had a great deal of talent; yes, I believe he was extraordinarily gifted, but he had a bad way of blaming other people for his own mistakes. He lost out once in a music competition, and he blamed it on the way things were run; you couldn't beat the system, he said, and he went into something safe, shielded himself from any further pain. But finally, after many years, he began to wonder what would have happened if he had tried again, if he had persisted and refused to accept a first disappointment—or even a second and third. Now the young man is getting old and he'll never have the answer; the only thing left of his great gift is the safe and empty comfort that he didn't really try."

Deborah's heart was full. She knew, without really knowing, that Mr. Stewart had told his own story. She wanted terribly to make some gesture toward him, tell him she understood and was sorry, promise him that she would always remember what he had said; but Mr. Stewart turned brusque again, and pointed to the white paper before her.

"I think you better begin on that," he said.

She lifted her pencil, thought for a moment, and then in a surge the words began to come.

When she walked out of his office she had the floating feeling again. The application would go in today, and Mr. Stewart had assured her she would know the date of the audition within a week; that is, if she lived that long, if she could pass the time without going mad. Then she thought of Steve. Oh, how wonderful this day was! Music, and Steve. All the doubts she had had about him vanished. She loved him and she was sure he loved her too. What more could she want or ask for?

She was still in this mood when she climbed into his car after school. It was one of those rare February days when the sun had awakened and stretched, casting its bright rays at patches of hardened snow, loosening them and penetrating the crisp, dry air with warm and fragrant moisture. It was the kind of day where you left off scarves and even hats, and breathed in the promise of springtime. Houses swam in sunlight and, as they drove past, she had the urge to be in the country again, to see the limp and saturated cornfields bathed in warm light. Steve took the road that led out of town and she leaned back in the seat, stretching lazily. "Mmmmm," she said, "I feel like being driven for hours while I float like a lily pad." She tugged at his arm and pointed to the empty spaces of land, near the edge of town, that were moving sedately by them now. "The snow is really beginning to melt," she said. "Pretty soon we'll be able to walk on the beach and in the park and out into the country . . . oh, I'll feel so free. Won't you?"

He turned his face from the road to smile at her. The familiar tingle went through her; but when he answered "Yep" in a flat and detached manner, the moment was lost.

"You don't sound very convincing," she said. "Don't you like the spring? Just think! We'll be able to picnic somewhere and I can watch you paint."

"Debby," he said, and his tone clearly indicated that he had not heard a word she had spoken. There was also something portentous about the sound of his voice that made her draw back inside herself as though the sunlight had been suddenly eclipsed and winter grayness were descending once more.

"Yes?" she answered.

"I've been accepted at Yale."

The words fell like a stunning blow and she could not answer at once, but after a moment she said flatly, "Congratulations."

"Don't be sarcastic."

"I didn't mean to be sarcastic . . . but, well, maybe I did mean it that way. Did you expect me to say I'm glad, considering how you felt about it before?"

"I had a talk with my folks, Deb."

She sat very still, hardly daring to breathe while he was

hesitating. This was what she had waited for—the moment that would exonerate everything they had done, the hiding and the white lies, the crouching feeling she had inside herself, and the sense of smallness she felt beside Pat Hamilton. She had never been able to bring herself to completely condemn Pat because she had not felt free enough of wrongdoing herself. She knew that Pat hated her from the very first for all the wrong reasons; but if that had not been so, if Pat had met her equally and fairly, she might have more readily conceded her now as the injured party. But Steve's answer now could bring an end to deceit; hereafter her relationship with Steve would be honest and open, and somehow she would make it up to anyone she hurt because of loving him.

"It's going to be hard to explain," Steve said, steering the car with one hand while he pulled a cigarette from his pocket and lit up. She had never seen him smoke before and it added to the aura of unpredictability, the rocking-horse effect of being up one moment and down the next.

"My folks don't change easily," Steve said. "They are what they are, I guess. They'll send me to Yale but not to art school; art doesn't fit in with the plan. It's okay with Dad if I insist on playing around with it; he even offered to keep me in paints, but art can't be the goal—not if the old man pays the bill."

She started to say "I see," but he interrupted her.

"I know what you're thinking, but don't be too hard on

185

them. They see things differently, and maybe they're right. I haven't had their experience, so how can I expect to know the answers?"

"You know what you want, don't you? At least you said you knew what you wanted. Why, all of a sudden, is it so unimportant? And even if you go to Yale, does it have to be law? Can't it be something you like?"

"It has to be law. The old man pays the bills and the firm has to stay in the family."

She whistled softly through her teeth. "Jumping cats, have you been brainwashed!"

"Okay, Deb, come off it. Have you got any smart suggestions about who might pay the bill? Any offers to keep Saint Steven in food and clothes while he suffers for art?"

"What if you decided to pay the bill yourself? Have you ever worked, Steve? I know a boy on the South Side who's worked since he was in the fifth grade. It doesn't scare him; nothing scares him—not the world, nor the big people in it who cluck, cluck and say you can't do what you're cut out for."

"He's lucky," Steve said—and, while he crushed his cigarette out in the ash tray, she thought to herself how laughable it was to call Tony Mescuto lucky. Tony, honor graduate of settlement houses and fresh-air camps, would consider Steve Randall the luckiest guy alive.

"Anyway," Steve went on, "I wish you'd cut this out. I might make a good lawyer at that, and the risks are practically nil. The firm has been going at a high clip for two generations; my grandfather built it up and I guess there's no chance of my wrecking it, no matter what I do."

She was certain now that his parents' answer where she was concerned had not changed either. He did not have to say it. There was not the ghost of a chance that the Randalls had suddenly decided to accept a Jewish girl, invite her to their home, or make Steve feel anything but guilty if he saw her on the outside. A Jewish girl didn't fit into the plan any more than Steve's leaving the family firm.

But what had he answered them? Had he taken the easy way out with this too? She felt a fatigue descend upon her, making her feel washed out and limp. She could not stand hearing him say he wasn't allowed to fall in love with a Jew, in the same resigned and accepting tone as he had said he was going to Yale.

Steve pulled the car over to the side of the deserted country road and switched off the ignition. They looked at each other; and before she knew what was happening she was in his arms, and the automatic drum inside her began its steady beat. She felt his lips on her eyes and mouth, and his arms held her so tight against him that she forgot for a moment the unanswered question between them, the mounting barriers that were pushing them apart. She opened her eyes and traced the outlines of his shoulders with her finger tips. It troubled her that it was only now, when he held her, that she loved him, and that all the other times, with the exception of the

187

time he showed her his paintings, she felt either annoyed or anxious.

"I love you, Debby," he said, and she felt peculiarly unresponsive as though someone had doused a light inside of her.

"Baby," he whispered, "none of what I told you counts for us. We go on and no one can stop us."

She pulled away from him. "How?" she asked. "In this car? Forever, like this?"

"No. I'll come to your house. I really want to."

"Steve," she said softly, "can I come to your house too?"

His eyebrows knit together tightly. "Why does that matter? I don't see why it's important."

"But telling your parents that you're seeing me, whether they approve or not, *is* important. Can't you understand that? Then it won't matter if I come to your house . . . just as long as they know. Just as long as we stop lying."

"You want everything," he answered gruffly. "It's not enough that I'm willing to risk their finding out—"

"No, Steve—no!"

"But my parents never have to find out," he repeated.

"Oh, Steve, I just can't make you understand. All right then. What happens when it comes time for the senior dance? If you don't take Pat, she'll snitch on you. Then what? Will you ask me to hide at home again while you take her?"

"You make it awfully hard, Debby. I'm beginning to wonder if you really love me."

It was a long moment before she answered, and then she averted her eyes from his face. If she looked at his lean, handsome features, at his deep blue eyes and shock of thick, blond hair, at the way his jaw set when he was listening intently, she could tell him only that she loved the feel of his face on hers, and the pressure of his arms around her. She had to look away from him to say it.

"I don't know, Steve. I'm mixed up about it. I only know I can't keep on feeling like a thief. For the first time in months, today, I felt proud of myself; and I felt as though I had earned another person's respect. If I started lying again or even letting you lie about me, it would spoil things. Don't you see? I'm not the girl you painted in the portrait, Steve; no, listen—I looked at it when I got home from Jessie's, and it didn't look like me at all. I stared at it, and the girl that stared back was a stranger. I'm not like her, Steve; she looks so . . . well, so small and lost and a little wild and irresponsible. Maybe I was like that when you painted me, but I don't feel that way any more."

He reached for her arm; but she pulled away, shaking her head.

"Please take me home, Steve. My feet are freezing."

The ride back, she thought, was the way people rode to funerals, aware of one another, the sadness and pain hovering silently, but conversation out of place and awkward. She was not sure that things between them were final and, if they were, she could not think about it; she had to keep her mind on something else. Steve was too close for her to imagine his never being close again. If

189

only she could confide in someone! Before, she had wanted desperately to talk to Mother, then Mark, then Midge, then even Stella; but she never had. Something had always stopped her. It was the first important thing that had ever happened to her that she had gone through by herself, completely alone; and now there was no point in telling anyone. A year ago she could not have done it; she could not have gone through anything without telling Mother, or at least Midge. But a year ago was a time in another world.

The car rounded a corner and she felt numb. In a moment she would get out and then it would be final. She glanced at Steve's solemn face furtively, almost in panic; there were things yet to be said, and neither of them had spoken.

He pulled up in front of her house and she opened the door. When she felt his hand on hers she winced, but she did not look at him.

"Debby," he said, and there was pain in his voice, "we'll talk again, won't we? We'll get together in school?"

"Sure," she interrupted him, and pulled her hand away. "We'll both have to go to school."

Then she was out of the car, and the sound of his motor died in her heart when she opened the front door of her house.

It was warm and light inside, and the aroma of freshly baked bread tickled at her nostrils and made her inhale deeply.

She closed the door with deliberate quiet so she could

190

get to her room without seeing anyone, but Grandpa was there in the hall holding a book at his side, observing her as if he had been doing it all day—all year. Their eyes met and she thought she had never seen his face so mellow or soft, or heard his voice so tender as he called to her in a near whisper. "Deborah. Perhaps after dinner you will play chess with your grandfather again? I am a little lonely today, and anyway, my old heart tells me you will win this time."

She started at his mention of chess but continued to stare at him, watching the folds of his face play into the yellowing beard. His blue eyes were misty as though he knew all that had taken place this day and had wept for her with both joy and sadness.

"Grandpa—oh, Grandpa." She was leaning against him now, crying with a full heart and he was stroking her hair with his long, gentle fingers.

"You see, Deborah," he chuckled, fingering a strand of her hair, "I told you, didn't I, that you couldn't stop it from growing?"